THE BILLIONAIRE'S UNWELCOME HOME

TAYLA ALEXANDRA

DEDICATION

Thank you to the One who gives His grace freely.

ALSO BY TAYLA ALEXANDRA

All Titles by Tayla Alexandra

<u>Her Sweet Billionaire Romance Series</u>
Her Billionaire Dream
Her Billionaire Jackpot
Her Billionaire Wish
Her Billionaire Chauffeur
Her Billionaire Scoundrel
To Trust Again - A novella

<u>Finding Trust Series</u>
Finding Alissa
Loving Josie
Reclaiming Bailey
Chasing Kennedy

A Billionaire's Tale Romance Series
The Billionaire Recluse
The Cinderella Ball

A Billionaire's Tale Romance Series
The Billionaire Recluse
The Cinderella Ball

Bucket list Billionaire Multi-author Series
Beached with a Billionaire

GET TAYLA ALEXANDRA'S STARTER LIBRARY FOR FREE

Sign up for my no spam newsletter and get the novella – *To Trust Again,* the Christmas short *Wrapped in Love,* and Brother of the Bride (Companion to The Cowboy's Forbidden Bride) and lots more exclusive content, all for free.

Details can be found at the end of the book.

PROLOGUE - 6 YEARS EARLIER

Jesse noticed Maya as soon as she strolled into the banquet hall. How could he not? No man, woman, or child for miles around could have missed her in that light blue evening gown that perfectly shaped her figure. And if they said they did, they were lying.

Although Maya carried herself as if she were nothing special, she was a beauty beyond compare. Maybe that was part of her appeal, he decided as he watched her chat easily with her friends. Maya prided herself on being book smart, but there was so much more to her than that.

Jesse had been talking to his date, minding his own business, but the moment she and her friends entered, he hadn't been able to take his eyes or mind off of her.

After watching her from the corner of his eye for the past half hour to make sure she hadn't come with anyone, he had to hide a smile. She had come stag and was hanging out with her friends. At the moment, she was at the back of the auditorium where she and her three friends were all talking in whispers.

Dance music bounced from the speakers and volleyed around the room, placing everyone in the mood to dance. Everyone except for Jesse. He eyed the room, thinking about Maya, stealing glances at her whenever he could without attracting attention to himself.

He couldn't believe it was now junior prom, and he hadn't spoken to Maya in weeks. He'd seen her on several occasions but was too chicken to ask her to go with him. That and there was the minor detail that he was dating someone else.

Jesse glanced at Tina for a moment and drew in a breath. Although he cared about Tina, he felt nothing more for her than friendship. The way he felt about the two girls in his life was like the difference between night and day.

He'd loved Maya from the first time he laid eyes on her. She was so shy, sweet, and smart like nothing he'd ever known or any other girl he'd ever met.

But Maya Brown was off-limits. She was poor, black, and had no future — Those were the exact words his father had used when he'd caught them kissing only a couple of weeks before. Jesse winced at the memory. He had wanted to kill his father that day for uttering those words, let alone calling him out in front of Maya.

His father only cared about one thing - money. And he believed if you had enough of it, you could say or do anything you wanted, no matter how despicable it was.

Maya looked his way briefly, then turned back to her friends. Jesse's heart hammered in his chest as he sucked down another glass of gin-spiked punch.

"Whatcha looking at?" Doyle, Jesse's buddy, asked. "Ah!" he said when his eyes found the same spot. "I dare you to walk over there and ask her to dance." Doyle shouldered him. "You know you want to."

"Shut up, Doyle. It's not like that." Of course Jesse wanted to ask her to dance, but not out of some sick desire to make a fool out of her. Doyle was a troublemaker and by all rights so was Jesse. Together they'd pulled more pranks than anyone in the history of Trust, Arizona. They'd stolen cars just for the fun of it, egged houses, shattered windows, broken into buildings... most of which while they were inebriated or high. Half the town was wary of Jesse and Doyle's antics, the other half just shook their heads and looked away as if too afraid to take on the billionaire brat pack.

Neither of them cared, though. Their fathers would pay for the damages, get them off the hook, give them a stern lecture followed by a beating and a promise to ship them off to boarding school if they didn't straighten up. But Jesse never believed his father would do it.

Their fathers were the richest, most prominent men in town, and Jesse could do or have whatever he wanted… except for the one thing in the world he desired most - Maya Brown. Jesse's reaction to Maya was so overwhelming that it sparked every electron in his body at the mere thought of her. His heart warmed. She was the last person he ever wanted to hurt. She made him want to be a different person.

"Hurry before she gets away," Doyle taunted, elbowing Jesse in Maya's direction.

"Shut up, Doyle." Tina punched Doyle on the arm. "Why are you always trying to start trouble?"

Maya turned in their direction, a shy smile shining on her face. Jesse's pulse quickened at the sight. Quiet energy swirled around him as if he were at the Superbowl, waiting for the game-ending field goal to be kicked. Only at that moment, Jesse was the kicker. He had the ball in his hands and the field goal was in sight. All he had to do now was make the score.

Maya frowned and turned back to her friends, but her warm, honey-brown face was still visible, and it sent tingles down Jesse's spine. Jesse stared, mesmerized. Her lips moved as she spoke, so full and sweet, making Jesse remember the moment they had shared.

His heart thumped, their only kiss etched in the back of his brain. No matter how he tried to remove it, forget it, play it off as nothing… it invaded his body, his being, making him long to touch her sweet lips just one more time. Jesse refused to look away even as the harsh words his father uttered after catching him at the tail end of a kiss rang through his head.

"You have no idea what love is." His father's twisted face flashed through Jesse's memory. He'd never forget how his dad's skin flushed and he raised a fist when he said, "You'll not ruin my reputation with that trash!"

Jesse took a step forward, determined not to let his father get the best of them, and at the very least apologize for how Maya had been treated that day. Jesse had been so embarrassed when his father had walked in and caught them off guard that he hadn't gotten the nerve to apologize. The second his father had started in, Maya had packed up her books and rushed out the door. She didn't know that if it hadn't been for his mother, he and his father would have come to blows that day. As it was, the stress level in the James' household was at an all-time high since the incident. Jesse was biding his time before he officially turned eighteen and could leave his father's home.

"Jesse?" The voice was faintly recognizable as Tina's, but Jesse couldn't think about her now. Maya deserved an apology, and Jesse was no better than his bigot father if he dared stand back any longer, pretending their kiss meant nothing.

It had been two weeks and Jesse had not spoken a word to her since. Two weeks of seeing her in school, watching her pretend she wasn't hurt each time their eyes met. Two weeks of dreaming things were different and that his father hadn't — Jesse took another step closer.

At that moment, the music stopped and couples exited the dance floor. Jesse's pulse quickened, and suddenly, the surrounding air seemed to thicken. When the DJ announced a slow song and more couples moved for the floor, passing those on their way back to their seats, Jesse's chest constricted. It was now or never.

His father came to mind, but Jesse pushed him to the back. What did it matter what color her skin was or how little money her father made? They weren't living in the dark-ages.

Jesse started in Maya's direction. This time, he would not stop. No hesitation. No regrets.

Doyle rubbed his hands together with a chuckle. He was getting too much fulfillment out of this, but Jesse was too focused on the mission at hand to care.

"Jesse James, if you ask her to dance, I will never speak to you again." The hurt in Tina's voice almost stopped him dead in his tracks — almost.

"Just one dance. I just want to apologize, that's all." That was a lie if he ever told one. No one in hearing range believed him. Certainly not Tina.

"Jesse," Tina glowered. "You don't owe her an apology. Isn't it enough that she even gets to attend our school?"

"What's that supposed to mean?" Jesse swiveled around to face Tina.

"Well, she is on scholarship."

"And?"

"And what? She's… Jesse, all I'm saying is, she's not our kind." Tina pointed a finger at him, her fake nail jabbing in his direction.

Without another word, Jesse turned his back on Tina. He'd never known she felt that way. Then again, although the town was multicultural, the school was anything but. It comprised at least ninety-seven percent Caucasian. Maybe more.

Tina puckered her lips into a pout as she glared at Jesse.

Maybe it wouldn't be such a bad thing if Tina never spoke to me again. Jesse raised a brow in her direction before turning his back on her.

Besides, Tina knew Jesse had a thing for Maya. Heck, everyone knew. Everyone except Maya. But the entire town also knew that Jesse's father was a bigot. Weiland James was a racist, sexist, powerful bigot who could tear a person to shreds with the snap of his fingers, and his son was no exception.

Although Jesse stood to lose a lot, his heart beat wildly in his chest as he took another step toward Maya, who was standing only three table-lengths away.

Jesse took another step in her direction, wondering if she thought of him at all. To him, she was more beautiful than any other girl in the room. Her shoulder-length, black hair, that was usually pulled back in a bun, was curled into ringlets around her face that made her look like a Nubian princess.

Maya looked up, her light brown eyes sparkling. When she caught him staring at her, she turned away before he could hold her gaze and hopefully convey something — anything. Ever since that kiss they'd shared, Maya had avoided him at all costs. He didn't blame her, really. She'd been afraid of his father. Everyone was afraid of Weiland James, including his own wife. But Jesse wasn't. He was tired of getting pushed around, being told what to do, how to think, who to love ...

"Jesse!" Tina spoke through pinched lips as she yanked the back of his suit jacket. "Please!"

"I'll be right back." Jesse moved her hand away and continued in Maya's direction.

"Go get 'er!" Doyle called, and then there was a sound of an oomph as Tina obviously punched him in the gut.

Jesse could have stayed and defended his friend, but he had to get to Maya. Nothing would stop him from his mission. Not Tina, not his father, not even Doyle, who was egging him on for no good reason. Jesse swallowed and pushed forward, thinking the spiked punch he'd drank too much of could have helped loosen his inhibitions. Either way, no matter the outcome, he pressed on regardless of any consequences.

A few more steps and he was at her side. Suddenly, all the words he'd planned to say fell silent. He'd wanted to tell her how beautiful she was, how he didn't care what his father said or that she was not wealthy. He wanted to tell her he loved her. That he'd loved her from the first moment he'd laid eyes on her when his mother hired her to tutor him three years ago. He wanted to tell her that being her friend wasn't enough. Jesse wanted her, needed her, and if he had his way, he'd spend the rest of his life with her. But none of that surfaced. Instead, he stood there and stared at her like an idiot.

"Did you need something, Jesse?" Maya asked.

"Hi, Jesse." Maya's friend, Sally, gave a two-finger wave and giggled, making Jesse smile.

"Hey, Sally." Jesse acknowledged, then turned to Maya. "I thought maybe you'd like to dance?" He held out a hopeful hand to her.

Maya glanced at him as if searching his face for sincerity. As their eyes connected, Jesse sucked in a breath, unable to get past how gorgeous she was. While he'd never seen her in anything other than jeans, seeing her now was far from a disappointment. She was the most stunning girl in the room.

Jesse had visualized her sweet face night after night in his dreams. He'd kissed her lips a thousand times when his eyes were closed. Each time, longing for more. Now, as he stood this close, all he desired was to hold her in his arms.

Maya took his hand with hesitation. "Are you sure about this?"

"What's there to be sure of? It's just a dance," he answered, knowing it was much more.

The second they stepped onto the dance floor, hand-in-hand, it took them to an entirely new realm - their hearts and souls becoming one.

Jesse held his head high. It didn't matter who saw them, or who knew, or who would tell his father what he had done. All that mattered was that they were together. And they stayed together that night and on into the next morning.

When Jesse awoke in the guest house, the first thing he noticed was Maya struggling to gather her belongings as their worlds came crashing down on them. That morning, they shipped Jesse James away from his hometown, and he would not return for a long, long time.

1

______

MAYA

Maya Brown kneeled down before her five-year-old son, Benjamin, and smiled. "You almost got it right, buddy. Give it one more try. This time, pull a little tighter."

Benjamin slumped his shoulders and tried tying his shoes one more time. "You do it much better, Mommy. Mine always comes undone."

"Practice makes perfect." Maya ruffled his soft, brown curls. "One more time. Mommy's going to be late for work if you don't hurry."

"Will mean Mr. James make you work late again if you're not on time?" Benjamin had never met his grandfather. Mean Mr. James did not know Benjamin's existence. Little Benjamin was Maya's best kept secret.

"Now, Benjamin." Maya tried to reprimand her son, but she could hardly blame him for speaking the truth. "Mr. James is not *always* mean. He did give Mommy a job, right?"

"I guess so." Benjamin pulled his laces tight, but even after all of his effort, they still flopped loosely to the ground. "He should let you come to work whenever you want."

Maya tied her son's shoes for him and then pulled the loops into a double knot. "What kind of world would it be if everyone could just come and go whenever they wanted?"

Benjamin giggled, making Maya wish she could spend the day with him instead of working on a Saturday. But she owed the James family too much to press the issue. "Mrs. James will be here soon. You enjoy spending the day with her, don't you?"

"She's fun, Mommy. But how come I never get to meet Mr. James?"

"You don't want to meet him." Maya lowered her brows and growled like a bear. "He's just an old grump, anyway."

Benjamin giggled as she kissed his nose.

No, she was the one who would have to deal with the ornery man. Better her than Benjamin, though. And Maya would do anything for her son. He was the one and only good thing in her life. If it meant sucking up to rich, white folks so that her son had everything he needed, that was what she would do. Besides, she and Claire James had forged the deal before Benjamin was ever born — Mrs. James would take care of Benjamin's every need and Maya would keep her mouth shut about who his father was. Mr. James would never know he was a grandfather. And Jesse — he would never find out he had a son.

It broke Maya's heart to keep Benjamin away from Jesse, but being that she hadn't seen him since the night they'd conceived, almost six years before, Maya had no other choice. It was what it was, and Maya had no right to put her son through poverty just because she still harbored a crush for his father. If Jesse James had wanted to be with her, he'd have found a way. Maya hadn't gone anywhere. She was still stuck in the same small town of Trust, Arizona, living her life under the rules and restrictions of Jesse's mother.

The doorbell rang.

"Hurry, hurry." Maya rushed Benjamin to the door. "We don't want to keep Mrs. James waiting."

Benjamin grabbed his backpack from the hook by the door and flopped it over his shoulder. He loved his grandmother, even if he didn't know who she was to him. And although Mrs. James adored him too, she refused to divulge the information to anyone that her family's twenty-four karat blood was tainted with African-American blood.

Although his light brown hair was filled with soft curls, his skin was as warm as honey, and his eyes held a tinge of green like his father's, the truth was not to be spoken. From the day he was born, Benjamin had been taken care of, spoiled with whatever he wanted and needed, and would always have the best of everything. He would only miss one small thing — a father.

"Good morning, Master Benjamin." Constance, Mrs. James's personal assistant, smiled at the boy. "Mrs. James is waiting for her favorite little boy in the car. Are we ready?"

Benjamin nodded heartily. Mrs. James would spend the day spoiling Benjamin, while Maya spent it working for Mr. James.

"Good. Come along, then." Constance took Benjamin's hand. "Your car will be here shortly." Constance nodded to Maya. Although Constance was as black as Maya was, Constance looked down on Maya as well. Maybe it was because Maya had stepped over the line by getting involved with a rich, white boy. Constance closed the door behind them, leaving Maya to stare at her surroundings. One night. One stupid night, and Maya's life had changed forever. And the worst part about it was that Maya had known better. Her mother had warned her from the very beginning.

"White people don't understand, Maya. They think, just because slavery has been over for all these years, that there is no racism in the world." Her mother had tried to explain that to her, but Maya had not understood. "And some people just don't like the idea of races mixing."

"Why are we any different? What does it matter? Aren't we all the same on the inside?"

"Please, Maya. You do your job over there and come home. Don't go catching feelings for a boy you can never be good enough for."

But Maya had been young and stupid. She had never known true racism until the day when the entire school found out she was pregnant. Maya had been the product of ridicule ever since.

Although gossip spread about her and Jesse leaving the junior prom together, the rumors were squashed. And then she was labeled with derogatory names she'd rather not repeat. But those names still hurt her to this very day. And then the inevitable happened. Jesse's mother had gotten wind of her pregnancy and the next thing she knew, she was whisked off to some school for pregnant women and hadn't been allowed to come back until after Benjamin was born and she had graduated high school. They had hidden her away and taken care of her ever since.

A few minutes later, another car came to escort her to work. Unlike the limo with driver and all the amenities that came for Benjamin, Maya's car was a taxi. Grabbing her purse, Maya didn't let it get to her on that day any more than it had for the last five years. Reminding herself where she could be, she gave thanks for where she was.

"Good morning, Maya," Hailey said as Maya climbed inside. "Working on Saturday again?"

"I sure am. Looks like you got a hold of the Saturday shift too."

"Yep." Hailey pulled her messy blonde hair into a ponytail behind her head. "Baby needs diapers. Besides, no one tells Claire James no. Not that I work for her, but yeah, well, I guess just about everyone works for her in some capacity."

Maya laughed. She and Hailey had been fast friends from the day they met, and there was no baby that needed diapers.

It was funny how some people didn't pay attention to the color of a person's skin at all, where others, even in this day and age, it was all they could see. Racism went both ways, though. Just as many black people hated the whites. Over a hundred and fifty years had passed since slavery, and still, some people couldn't figure out how to get along.

Hailey pulled the taxi up to the towering James building, where dozens of ambulances and police cars idled outside.

"What's going on?" Maya asked, leaning forward in her seat.

"Looks like someone must have gotten hurt." Hailey placed the car in park. "I hope it wasn't one of those homeless guys who like to sleep on the bench out front. I heard—" She stopped mid-sentence. "Wait! Is that Mr. James?"

Maya scooted on to the edge of her seat and squinted out the window as EMTs pushed a gurney with an overweight, pale, white man strapped to the bed. Maya clasped her hand over her mouth. "That *is* Mr. James!"

"Is he dead?" Hailey's eyes were as big as cannonballs.

"I sure hope not!" She'd never wished a person dead in her entire life. Still, she wondered, would things change if Mr. James were... dead?

"What do we do? Should I just drop you off here?" Hailey looked back at Maya, who was still staring in stunned silence at Mr. James, who was being loaded into an ambulance. "Or do I take you back home?"

"Uh... I don't know."

2

———

JESSE

Jesse James yawned as he pulled his Jeep Wrangler into the barracks parking lot. After twelve hours in the ER, he was beyond tired. At least he would be off for a couple of days before his next shift.

Becoming a Hospital Corpsman in the United States Navy had been Jesse's way of getting away from his father after the man had sent him off to boarding school the summer after his junior year of high school. He'd learned that it didn't matter how much money his family owned, Jesse was a petty officer second class in the United States Navy. They gave him no special treatment from anyone, and no one knew that his family was worth billions of dollars. To the Navy, he was just - HC2 James and that was what he preferred. No one washed his clothes for him or pressed and ironed them. No one waited on him hand and foot, drove him places, cooked and cleaned for him, shined his shoes, nor many of the other menial chores he'd grown up used to others doing for him. In fact, Jesse had seen days where he'd overspent his menial paycheck and ended up eating ramen noodles or standing in line at the galley just to get a bite to eat. Not once had he thought of calling home and groveling for money.

Learning how to fend for himself had been the most freeing thing Jesse had ever done. And now that he was relieved from the stress of his father, he vowed to never go back. Besides his mother, who he missed dearly, there was only one person in that town that he ever wanted to see again, and that was Maya. She was his heart. His love. No one would ever replace her. But Maya was gone. His mother had told him so. Only a few months after being whisked off to boarding school, Maya and her family had left town and no one had seen or heard from her since.

Jesse wondered for a long time what had happened to her. He'd even done a little research but came up with nothing about where she could have gone. He'd even come home for break that year, but even though he'd asked around, no one knew where she'd gone. It was like she'd just disappeared. And along with it, she'd taken his heart. That was when he'd left. In the words of his father - he'd shamed his entire family. His father refused to speak to him, and his mother... sadly she'd gone along with him. Weiland James was not someone to be questioned, and he was not someone who forgot easily.

When Jesse joined the military, he made sure no one knew about it. He'd joined straight from boarding school the summer he'd graduated, and came back to find out that Maya had left. Of course, if they wanted to, his family could find him. It didn't take much to find an active duty military member if you had their social security number. But no one had even looked for him. Not his mother or his father, not even Maya.

"What's up, man?" Patrick, Jesse's roommate, asked as soon as Jesse came through the door. "Three days off. I say we head out to the south for a little party action."

Being stationed on the island of Guam for over a year, Jesse was used to the power outages, load-shedding, and constant feeling of dampness in the air. But the parties on the south side of the island, those things could go on for days. "I'm going to pass this time, man. You go on without me."

"What are you going to do? Sit and rot in the barracks for three days?"

"What's wrong with that?" Jesse flopped down onto his bed. "I'm tired."

Before Patrick could answer, a knock came at the door. "You expecting someone?"

"Nope." Jesse sat up. "You gonna answer it?"

Patrick went to the door. "Look, man. If you don't go, I'll have to find a ride."

"So the truth comes out at last." Jesse rolled his eyes. "You're using me for my ride."

"No." Patrick opened the door. "That's not all. You're a chick-magnet too - oh, hey, Stanley. Wanna go to a party in Tamuning?"

"Is Petty Officer James here?" Petty Officer Stanley asked. "The Command Master Chief wants to see him ASAP."

"Great." Jesse got out of his bed. "What did I do now?"

"I don't know, but you better get there fast. He's not happy that he had to come in on a Saturday as it is. He's at the quarterdeck."

Jesse hadn't gotten the chance to change out of his work uniform, so he jammed back on his chukkas and headed to the door. "Be back in a bit," he called as he headed down to the quarterdeck. The Command Master Chief didn't scare him. Anyone who grew up with a father like Weiland James did not scare easily.

Jesse took the stairs to the quarterdeck two at a time and landed with a thud at the bottom after jumping the last five. A couple of girls giggled as he stood grinning from ear to ear. He was a woman magnet alright, but try as he might to date, there was only one who held his interest, and she was gone.

"You wanted to see me, Master Chief?" Jesse asked, stepping up to the counter.

"Come back to my office, Petty Officer James." Master Chief Wilder grabbed his coffee-stained mug, filled it to the top with black sludge, and slapped Jesse on the back. "You got some explaining to do."

Without another word, Jesse followed the master chief into his office that was no bigger than a large closet. He sat across from the man as he did over a year before when he'd come to Naval Base Guam and then again when he'd made second class and one other time when he'd gotten into a minor scuffle out in town. Each time, Master Chief Wilder had spoken to him as if he knew him well. Now, as the two stood across from each other, MC Wilder stared at Jesse as if he didn't know him at all.

"Have a seat, James." Master Chief Wilder squeezed around his desk and plopped down into his chair. Being overweight seemed to be a rank thing. Once you made chief, no one seemed to care if you put on a few pounds.

Jesse sat. "What brings you in on a Saturday?"

Master Chief Wilder pulled out the file that he'd tucked under his arm all this time and slapped it onto the table in front of him. He set his coffee mug down next to it. "It seems you have a family emergency, Petty Officer James." Master Chief eyed him as if saying - why don't you already know about this?

"A family emergency?"

"Seems your father - one Weiland James, is in the hospital." Master Chief folded his hands and placed them on the desk. Clearing his throat, he said, "Billionaire Weiland James."

Jesse did not bat an eye. He'd hated his father for as long as he could remember. Him being in the hospital changed nothing. "Okay."

Master Chief Wilder stared at Jesse as if he was crazy. "Let me get this straight." Placing his fingers into a teepee, he leaned his chin on top and gave Jesse a smirk. "Your father is Weiland James, the multi-billionaire. Is this correct?"

Jesse nodded his head.

"And you, Jesse James, are a petty officer in the United States Navy."

Jesse nodded again.

Master Chief stood and slapped his hands on the table. "Why?"

Jesse watched the man. "Why what?"

"Why?" Master Chief Wilder threw his hands in the air. "Why on God's green earth would you join the navy in the first place, son? Your father is a billionaire! That makes you a billionaire!"

"I guess so." Although that observation was the farthest thing from the truth, Jesse didn't argue. No one seemed to understand that just because his father was rich, did not mean that Jesse was automatically wealthy. That was probably what it should mean, or meant among 'normal' families, but Jesse's family was far from normal. Weiland James worked hard for every dime he made and he wasn't about to just pass it down because they shared the same DNA, and to be honest, Jesse was not interested in the complications that came with it.

Master Chief Wilder plopped back into his chair and rubbed his face. "I will never understand your generation." He stared at the wall for a moment. "Anyway. You have been granted emergency leave." He pulled an envelope from his basket marked — in — and slid it across the table. "Two weeks. Go home and take care of business, rich boy."

Jesse stared at the packet in front of him. "What if I don't want to take leave?"

"Look, Petty Officer James. My wife is making biscuits and gravy for breakfast this morning. My three boys are sitting around the table as we speak, waiting for their daddy to get home so they can eat. How long do you think they are going to wait for me before they dip their fingers into the gravy?"

"I don't want to take the leave. I'm not going." Jesse stood. "Enjoy your biscuits and gravy. Sorry to bring you out here on your day off."

"How did I not know this would happen?" MC Wilder sat back down with a sigh. "Look. I can't force you to take leave. Whatever's going on between you and Daddy Warbucks, you can keep that to yourself, but Imma tell you right now, if you don't make things right when you can, you'll regret it for the rest of your life."

Jesse nodded. He knew that, and he was prepared to deal with that guilt if he had to. Nothing, no amount of apologies would make up for what his father had done to him. Not ever.

"Fine. I'm going to leave this packet with the quarterdeck watch. If you change your mind, your flight out is tomorrow night. I've authorized the duty driver to escort you to the airport."

Jesse stood. "I won't be changing my mind. Thank you, Master Chief."

Master Chief Wilder shook his head, stood, and headed for the door. "Suit yourself. Just remember," He pointed a finger at Jesse. "Sometimes time changes our perspective. Whatever happened between you and your father could be water under the bridge. You never know unless you give it a chance."

Not willing to be disrespectful, Jesse thanked the master chief and left his office. Water under the bridge? It was possible his father had changed, but Jesse doubted it.

3

———

MAYA

Maya sat outside Mr. James' office, waiting to be told what to do. No word had come down yet as to why Mr. James had been carted away in an ambulance, and work seemed to carry on as usual. It was as if nothing had happened. All except for the fact that since Maya worked directly for Mr. James himself, and besides the few Saturday morning items he normally had her take care of, she had no idea what to do. She'd already completed his Saturday errands.

Before she could ponder calling Hailey back for a ride home, Mrs. James came trudging into the office with Benjamin in tow.

"Mommy!" Benjamin ran to Maya.

Maya grabbed him up, hugging him. "You okay?"

"Yes. Mrs. James said I have to stay with you while she goes to the hospital."

"Right." Maya looked up at Mrs. James, who was speaking animatedly on her cell phone. "Mr. James is sick, buddy."

"Why, Mommy?"

"Because——" Maya started to explain but stopped when she heard a bit of Mrs. James' conversation. "Have a seat, buddy."

"But, Mommy!"

"Shhh." Maya put her finger to his mouth as she listened.

"I need you here, son. Your father needs you... The past doesn't matter. He's sick, Jesse."

At the mere mention of his name, Maya trembled. Had Mrs. James known where he was this entire time?

Benjamin sat, staring at Maya as Maya stared at Mrs. James, waiting for the conversation to continue. Her heart thumped in her chest at the thought of Jesse being on the other end of the line. The past five years had been as if Jesse did not exist. It was rare to hear his name roll off of anyone's tongue, especially his father's.

"Do you care so little for your own father that you... Jesse, I will not allow you to talk to me like that. You get on that plane tomorrow, or I will send the jet to come get you, kicking and screaming if I have to."

Benjamin turned to Mrs. James, then went back to his mother. "She's mad, Mommy." Benjamin swallowed.

"Yes, honey." Maya pulled him closer. He wasn't used to hearing people raise their voices. "It's okay, honey."

Mrs. James smiled at Benjamin, then reached out and patted his head to assure him she was not angry with him. She and her son exchanged a few more choice words, and then Mrs. James hung up the phone.

"He'll be here by Monday evening."

Maya's nerves stood on end as she watched Mrs. James. Had she heard her right? "He's coming... home?"

"As of this moment, you no longer work for Mr. James. Do you understand me?" Mrs. James' voice was demanding, but not harsh.

"Is Mr. James okay?" Maya placed her arms around her son's shoulders.

"No. He's not." Mrs. James' voice matched her stern face. "He will not be back at work. Jesse will take over the company."

"Jesse?"

"Yes. And you will not be a distraction for him, do you understand?"

The universe swung wildly as Maya tried to stay on her feet. She swallowed and blinked to stop the spinning. Jesse was coming home?

And he was taking over his father's business? From the conversation she'd just overheard, it hadn't sounded like Jesse had agreed with that plan.

"What… where… I'm not sure I understand."

"Nothing has changed except that you will no longer work for Mr. James. Your apartment will still be paid, and Benjamin here will be well taken care of." Mrs. James smiled at Benjamin, gave his cheeks a little pinch, then looked back up to Maya. "You can take on another job if you like, but it's unnecessary."

"Where would I work?" Although Maya was well provided for, she'd not had any formal schooling past high school. Mrs. James had snuck her into the company right under her husband's nose. Maya had worked directly for him, and he didn't know that she'd given birth to his grandson or that she was the same person who had tutored his son years before. He'd never even made the connection between the girl he'd found in his guest house and the one who poured his coffee every single morning. No doubt she looked much different after the few pounds she'd put on giving birth, and then of course Mr. James had been too livid to find his son in bed with his arms wrapped around a black girl, to really look at Maya. It was his son who had disappointed him, and that was where his anger had lain.

"Get a job somewhere in your neighborhood if you like," Mrs. James said with a small wrinkle of her nose. "Just stay on that side of town and there will be no problem."

"Right." Maya's apartment wasn't in the worst part of town, but it wasn't anywhere near the rich part of town either. No one in the James family would have any reason to venture into her world. Mrs. James was the only one who knew where she lived. "Thank you, Mrs. James."

Mrs. James smiled down at her. "I know you understand, Maya. It's not that… I need Jesse to be focused when he comes home. It will overwhelm him enough to see his father so sick, but Jesse will have to take over for him. You understand, don't you?"

Maya cleared the lump in her throat. "Yes, Mrs. James. I understand." And she did. She understood that she was a lowly black woman with a mixed child born out of wedlock, and that whatever the James family did for her was out of pity and that she didn't deserve any of it. She understood that if she did not do as she was told, Benjamin, who had reached the age of five without ever knowing poverty, would see firsthand what it was like to want... need. All the love she felt for Jesse was not worth the damage she could do to her son by making his existence known.

Jesse had had plenty of time and opportunity to contact her. He hadn't. She had been nothing to him but a bet. She'd been subjected to all the rumors. Doyle Anderson had bet Jesse that he couldn't get the poor colored girl to dance with him. Jesse had won and gone the extra mile. Only his parents hadn't thought the bet was very funny. Imagine their surprise at finding a naked black girl in their guest house. And Jesse had just stood there as his father berated her, shamed her, spoke to her as if *she* had seduced *him*.

"Why don't you two head home?" Mrs. James kissed Benjamin on the cheek. She seemed to love the boy and Mrs. James had treated Maya well too. But Maya and Benjamin were Mrs. James' secret. As much as she 'loved' them, she was also ashamed of them. Maybe that was because of their color, or maybe it was the mere fact that Jesse and Maya had conceived a child out of wedlock. Or maybe it had nothing to do with any of that, and it was more about Mr. James and his tendency to uncontrollable outbursts. Either way, Maya was at the mercy of Mrs. James for as long as she wanted her son to have a good life. Nothing in the world meant more to Maya than Benjamin. Nothing.

4

____

JESSE

Jesse stood when the flight touched down in Phoenix, his head throbbing from the time change and lack of sleep. Why he even bothered to come was beyond him. Normally his mother's attempt at guilting him didn't work, but this time Jesse had given in. It wasn't what she had said about him making amends with his father, or even the fact that the man was on his deathbed. No, the only reason Jesse was coming home was because if his mother was right, and his father was really dying, Jesse would finally be free of the man.

It hurt worse than anything to know he felt so much animosity toward his father, but Weiland James had crossed the line. For Jesse's entire life, he'd suffered ridicule, mistreatment, and abuse from his father. But that last time when his father had caught him and Maya in the guest house and had treated her like she was some kind of black widow who had lured him into her web, Jesse had hated his father. Nothing the man could say or do would ever make Jesse change his mind about how he felt about the man. Not even on his deathbed could his father make amends. Because of his father, Jesse had lost the only person he'd ever loved more than himself.

Leaving the plane, Jesse robotically passed the gates, walked down the escalator to the baggage claim, lifted his olive green sea bag from the turnstile, and stopped in front of a black man holding a sign that said - *Mr. James.*

"Henry, you old bull! Still working for my father?" Jesse grinned wildly at his old friend.

"Master James." Henry nodded with a grin of his own. "It's good to see you. Let me get that for you." He reached for Jesse's bag.

"I got it, Henry. Relax." Henry had to be at least in his late sixties. For as long as Jesse had known the man, which was all his life, Henry had always seemed old to him.

"As you wish, Master James. Shall we head straight to the hospital?"

"Let's go home first. How's the old hypocrite doing, anyway?"

Henry's eyes grew wide, and then he let out a choked laugh. "Old grudges die hard, don't they?"

Why Henry ever worked for a bigot like Jesse's father, he would never understand. Weiland James was known for hiring most his home staff with African Americans. Many would find it as him being an equal opportunist, but Jesse saw it as only a show of power. Weiland James paid his workers well to be treated as second-class citizens. Money talked. For the right price, most people would do just about anything. Jesse was not most people, and he refused to be treated badly for one second by his father. Dying or not.

But Jesse James was no saint. There were other reasons he'd never come back to town. Too many to mention. Much of it was teenage pranks, running amok, and a general lack of supervision, but one huge thing had happened that night he'd spent with Maya in the guest house. One of his father's warehouses had been burned to the ground. Two security guards had died in that fire.

Jesse had been cleared of all charges, but his father still blamed him for it. As many times as Jesse had threatened to vandalize his father's property, it hadn't been him. Sometimes, he wondered if his father would have rather he had burned down the building than embarrassed him by being with Maya. At least then, he'd be able to control the situation.

Before Jesse could step foot in the home he grew up in, his phone rang. It was his mother. "Where are you? You should be here by now."

"I had Henry bring me to the house."

"Why would you do that? Jesse, your father is in critical condition."

"I'm tired, Mom. With the sixteen-hour flight and time change— "

"This is your father we are speaking of. He may not make it through the night."

Jesse tried to make himself care, for his mother's sake, but he just had no good feelings for his father.

"For me, Jesse, please. I need you here."

Those were the only words his mother could say that could force Jesse into compliance, and she knew it. His mother meant the world to him. "Okay, Mom. I'll be right there."

"Thank you, son. Take whichever car you like. Just ask Henry for the key to the lockbox."

"Okay. I'll be there soon." Jesse hung up and took a deep breath. He wasn't ready to see his father. Not under any circumstances. Somewhere deep inside, he knew it was wrong to wish his father to be gone before he got there, but he couldn't help wishing it, anyway. "Henry!" he called.

"Yes, Master Jesse?" Henry came from around the corner like an apparition.

"You don't have to call me that anymore, Henry. I'm grown now."

"Well, you were still a boy when you left. What shall I call you, then?"

"Jesse is fine. Henry, I have a question for you. Maybe you could give me an honest answer?"

"Of course, Master Jesse."

Jesse shrugged. It would take a long time before Henry stopped thinking of Jesse as a young boy. He'd grown up with Henry around more than his own father. "Henry, was I a bad kid?"

Henry lifted an eyebrow. "Is this a trick question, Master Jesse?"

"You know what I mean." Jesse let out a long sigh. "Was I that bad?"

"All things considered." Henry rubbed at his clean-shaven face. "You did nothing that can not be forgiven."

"Do you think Elvie would agree with that?" Elvira was the first nanny that Jesse remembered. He'd driven her crazy until finally, she quit.

"Ms. Elvira has forgiven you, I'm sure. What is all this about, anyway?"

Jesse shoved his hands into his pants pocket. "I don't know. I guess I'm just nervous about seeing my father again. Where are the keys to the truck?"

"The newest addition to your father's collection, or the classic Model TT?"

Jesse threw his head back and laughed. "I've missed you, Henry!"

His father had an old 1925 Model TT Farm truck that maxed out at about fifteen miles per hour. Jesse had snuck into his father's garage when he was about ten and took that baby for a spin around town. He hadn't gotten far before his father was notified, though. An old truck like that didn't escape notice for too long. Jesse had been duly punished with the beating of his life and a month grounding in which his father was too busy to notice if it were being adhered to. His mother had let him off after about a week. She was always the more lenient of the two. It was as if she was always making up for what his father lacked.

"I'll take the new truck. What year is it?"

"Next year's model. I'm sure you will enjoy it." Henry pulled a set of keys from his pocket, removed a single key and pushed the ring back into his pocket. "Your mother has advised me you are to have whatever you desire."

"Right." There were only two things in the world he desired. One was to see Maya again, and the other was to not have to see his father. He didn't suspect either of those wishes to come true anytime soon. "I better get to the hospital."

"Master Jesse?" Henry took a step closer. Placing a hand on

Jesse's shoulder, he said, "Go easy on him. Your father is very sick, and I think maybe he's a bit sorry, too."

"Sorry?" Jesse pretended as if he didn't know what Henry was speaking about. "You mean the father of the year? He has nothing to be sorry for."

Henry gave him a long stare. Giving in, he smiled. "If you say so, Master Jesse." Henry was the only person in the world who would give it to Jesse straight and not make excuses for his father. And here it seemed he was doing just that.

Gripping his lips tight, Jesse refused to pose the question that was on the tip of his tongue — Why are you even still here? Henry was well past retirement age and should be spending his time with his family. He had three children of his own who were all grown now and giving Henry several grandchildren he could be spoiling. But Henry's reason for staying around was none of Jesse's business.

Jesse shoved the garage lockbox key into his pocket and headed out. Stalling wouldn't change the fact that he would have to face his father sooner or later.

Choosing the keys for his father's brand new truck, Jesse jumped in and hit the button to open the third garage bay door. It had been a long time since Jesse had driven in anything newer than the old Jeep he'd purchased after bootcamp. He'd been determined to call home for nothing. He didn't want or need any help from his parents, and for the last six years, he'd not called once.

Jesse searched the steering wheel column for a place to put the key. There wasn't one. "What in the world?" He turned the fob around in his hand. It was not a key at all. It was nothing but a fob, and Jesse had no idea how to start the vehicle.

"Place your foot on the brake and press the button," Henry called from the bay entrance.

Jesse did as he was told, and the truck started right up. He shook his head. His father always did have to have the latest and greatest gadgets. Once upon a time, Jesse had wanted to be just like him. He wasn't sure when he'd gone from idolizing his father to hating him, but the process had most likely been a slow one.

The built in GPS directed Jesse to the hospital where his father had his own room secluded from the rest of the patients. Of course, they would not throw good ole Weiland James in with the common folk.

Jesse's mother looked up as he walked into the waiting room.

"How is he?"

"Oh, Jesse!" His mother rushed to him and pulled him into a tight hug. "I'm so glad you came." She looked as if she'd aged twenty years since he'd last seen her, and she'd lost weight too. She felt like skin and bones in his arms.

"How are you, Mom?" Jesse kissed his mother's cheek. He missed her more than he realized.

"I'm better now that you're here. Do you know what it took to find you?"

"Not much, I'm sure."

"Well, not really. I mean, I knew right away that you had joined the service. But getting ahold of your command to contact you, that was like pulling teeth. I think I talked to twenty different people before I finally spoke to someone who could help me." His mother let go and stood back.

"Well, here I am." Jesse stretched, feeling out of his element. It was so strange to be back home again. "Is he awake?"

His mother hadn't told him what was wrong with his father. The AMCROSS message Master Chief Wilder had shown him only said that his father was in critical condition. Not sure he wanted to know, he didn't ask.

"He's sleeping right now." His mother stepped closer. "I'm scared, Jesse."

"What happened?" He didn't want to know, but he couldn't leave his mother to bear the burden on her own.

"He just fell at work. He passed out. At first we thought it was just fatigue. Your father has been working so hard on this new merger. But then the doctor worried there was more to it. First, they thought he'd had a stroke, but now it turns out— " His mother let out a whimper, tearing his heart to pieces.

Jesse pulled her closer, wishing he could take the pain from her. "What is it?"

"A brain tumor." The shakiness in her normally sturdy voice scared him. His mother was not an emotional being. He'd never seen her so rattled in his life. She was usually the cool-headed one. The rational one. The glue that held everything together when it was falling apart. And now, she needed him.

Emotions crept up the back of his throat, and he bit it back. "I'm sorry, Mom."

5
______

MAYA

It was going on a week since Mr. James had entered the hospital and Maya had been essentially fired. Of course, she didn't have to worry about paying bills. They were all paid for. But she was going crazy being at home by herself all day.

Nothing had changed as far as Benjamin. A driver still came each day to take him to school and bring him home. Whether Mrs. James would still take him on their Saturday visits was yet to be seen since Maya hadn't heard a word since their last conversation.

What Maya wondered the most was whether Jesse had actually made it back home. Surely he'd have come to see his father. Maya glanced out the window, remembering the times she'd spent at the James house.

Although Mr. James had allowed Maya to tutor his son, he'd made it clear from the start that she was not welcome any farther than the kitchen, nor was she ever to come to their front door. He instructed her to arrive through the back service entrance just as the rest of their household staff. That had bothered Jesse more than it had her. Maya had been amazed to be in such a wondrous home to begin with. She'd been fascinated by all the pools, the basketball courts, tennis courts, and larger-than-life golf course. Never had she been past the kitchen as his father had demanded, but many times, Mrs. James had allowed them to sit outside next to the pool to study. The first time a servant had come and asked them what they would like to drink, Maya about flipped. Right away, she noticed that although Jesse had the world at his fingertips, he was far from happy.

And then they'd grown closer. Talking to each other about their hopes and dreams. He, wishing he could live the simple life and her promising to trade lives with him whenever he was ready.

"You think they would notice if we just switched?" he'd asked.

"Like *The Prince and the Pauper*?"

Maya had only been kidding, but Jesse had admonished her for speaking that way. "You are not a pauper." That was when he'd kissed her. "You're a —" He'd never finished that sentence because his father had come in just as their lips had parted and Maya was asked to leave.

That had been the last time she'd tutored him, but it hadn't been the last time they'd seen each other. Every day at school, Maya had seen him from afar, and every day she'd wished things were different. She'd even gone so far as to wish she wasn't black.

Maybe if she'd just been a poor white girl his father would have allowed them to see each other. Her mother had reprimanded her at the time, telling her she should never be ashamed of her color. "God made you who you are for a reason. Don't you go letting no bigot like Weiland James tell you that you are any less than he is."

But now her mother was gone and Maya had no one except for Mrs. James. And Benjamin. He was her lifeline. If only Mr. James knew he had such a handsome grandson. What would he do if he knew?

Mrs. James wasn't a bad person, really. She'd made the best of a bad situation, and she'd done everything she could to provide for Maya and Benjamin without Mr. James knowing. Maya didn't know what the man would do if he knew his secretary was the mother of his grandson.

Maya opened her laptop and checked her email. She'd put in several applications for jobs in the area. She didn't need the money, but she was driving herself crazy sitting around the apartment, dreaming about Jesse, wishing her life was different.

The second email from the top was from the coffee shop down the street. She'd filled out the application online and was hoping they'd call since it was one of the few businesses within walking distance.

Clicking open the email, Maya read it to discover she had an interview at one o'clock. She glanced at the time. It was almost one already. Maya rushed into the bathroom to freshen up and then headed for the door. Luckily for her, Benjamin was in full-day kindergarten and wouldn't be back for a couple more hours.

Five minutes later, and three minutes before one, Maya slipped inside *The Coffee Spot*. She'd been to the place at least a handful of times. The coffee was nothing compared to the expensive joint where she purchased Mr. James' coffee, but it was satisfactory, and the workers seemed happy.

"Hi. I'm here for an interview with your manager?" Maya spoke to the lady behind the counter who was helping another customer. "My name is Maya Brown."

The woman gave her a quick glance and then handed the customer an iced coffee. "The position is filled."

"What? I just…" Maya understood completely what that meant. "Yeah. Thanks anyway."

Maya stormed outside trying her best not to go off on the woman inside the shop. How had she never noticed before that every employee she'd seen inside when she got coffee had been white? As she paced herself back to her apartment, she tried not to get angry at a world that had come so far from racism yet still held nuances of hate that lingered in the air, reminding her that she was a subpar human.

Her phone rang, and she pulled it out. It was Hailey. Happy for the distraction, Maya answered. "Hi, Hails. What's up?"

"Hey, lady," Hailey answered. "Wanna get some coffee and talk about the latest gossip? I know a great place only a block from your house."

Maya groaned. "Coffee, yes. The one down the street — no."

Ten minutes later, Hailey had picked Maya up, and they drove to another coffee shop a little closer to the part of town where the rich dwelled.

"So, what happened? I thought you liked *The Coffee Spot*?"

Maya told Hailey about the interview she was scheduled for where the position was mysteriously filled.

"You really think stuff like that still happens?" Hailey asked, sitting in a booth across from Maya. "I mean, that's against the law, right?"

"Sure it is. Its racial discrimination. But of course she won't admit that she doesn't want a black woman working in her shop. It happens all the time."

"Why have I never noticed? I thought people all got along these days."

Maya let out a snort then covered her mouth. "You never noticed because you're white."

"No way!" Hailey stared at Maya. "Are you serious, because I know there are still people who are racist, but most people aren't… are they?"

"There's racism on all sides of the board. White people think black people are less than them. Black people think white people are too snooty. Asians think they're smarter than the rest of the world, and then there are Mexicans who -" Maya thought for a moment. "Oh, I guess Mexican's are cool." Who could put down Mexicans? Their food was the best.

"That's really not fair. I'm white, and I don't think like that at all."

"Yeah. You and me - we are the exceptions." It wasn't true. There were plenty of good people in the world who didn't care a bit what a person's skin color was. But if Maya had learned one thing in her life it was that the bad stood out in everything.

"I think there are more exceptions than you know." Hailey took a sip of her coffee. "Look at Mrs. James. She's really taken care of you and Benji."

"Don't get me started on that." Maya was in no mood to talk about the James' family at the moment.

"What? She pays for your apartment, food, utilities. She buys everything for you and Benji. I'm kind of envious."

"You don't get it, do you?" Maya took a sip of her coffee. "She's only taking care of us out of obligation. You know, she doesn't want to tarnish her family's good name."

"No way. You think so?"

Maya stared at Hailey, unspeaking. If the girl really thought Mrs. James was some kind of upstanding citizen for taking care of them, she was wrong. Mrs. James was doing what she did best. Sweeping James family issues under the rug was her sole job, and she did it well.

"No really. Why would she—"

"Why do you think Mr. James knows nothing about Benjamin? Do you even think Jesse knows he has a son?"

"No. Probably not. But you think that's the reason? I thought Jesse just ran away, and no one has been able to contact him?"

"He's back."

"What?"

"He's back," Maya repeated. "Or he should be soon. I heard Mrs. James talking to him. I'll bet you another cup of coffee that she's known where he's been this entire time."

Hailey stared at Maya in silence.

6

———

JESSE

Jesse stood at the back of the room and watched his father sleep. His mother had left him there hours ago, saying she had something to tend to. What, he didn't know, but his mother seemed to act a bit suspiciously. It was almost like she was hiding something. Then again, she'd been through a lot in the last couple of years dealing with his father all alone. No doubt she'd ended up getting the brunt of his verbal abuse, but his mother could handle herself. She always had.

Jesse leaned back on the wall. He loved his mother, but he didn't feel sorry for her. She could have left his father at any time and taken half of his fortune with her. In fact, Jesse's life might have turned out much differently if she had. But all of that was water under the bridge. Joining the navy had been the best thing he'd ever done. He'd learned a trade and had grown up significantly. The navy had turned an angry kid on a path to destruction into a reputable man. They'd taught him that life was far from fair and that he'd fared much better than the average person. His father had been harsh, but even worse than that, he'd been absent, leaving Jesse to figure out many things on his own. Where his father had left an enormous gaping hole, the navy had filled in and turned him into a man of integrity. That was something to be proud of.

But the one thing the navy couldn't do for him was make him forget Maya or forgive his father. The two went together, hand in hand. The only way he could ever forgive his father was if the man owned up to who he was — a hateful, racist, money-hungry…

"Is that my son, pouting against the wall?" His father's voice was gruff, startling him.

Jesse looked up. Steam rolled off the back of his neck as he stared into the eyes of the man who had caused him so much grief. After six years of not seeing his son, that was how he addressed him? Some things never changed. "Hey, Dad."

"Don't — Hey, Dad me." His father coughed and grabbed at his chest. "You have no right coming here after all the stress you caused to your mother."

"I caused?" That old bitterness slapped Jesse in the heart. He'd promised on the plane trip back to the states that he would not allow his father to get a rise out of him, but that was swiftly flying out the window. "Whatever, Dad. Good to see you, too."

Jesse stormed out of the room before his father could say another word. Why his mother had ever wanted him to come was beyond him. He and his father were like oil and water. If his father were to keel over right there and die, Jesse would not shed a single tear. He hated his father — plain and simple.

Darting out of the building, Jesse jumped into the truck, hit the button, and squealed out of the parking lot. Willing himself to calm down before he got into an accident, he tried to think of something else. But everything else he thought about brought him right back to his father.

"Slow down," Jesse coaxed himself to take his foot off the gas and slowly pressed the brake. "The last thing you want to do is crash his car."

Crashing his car actually didn't sound like such a bad idea. "Stop it." He let out a maniacal laugh. You're just— " Jesse slammed on the brakes as two women exited a nearby coffee shop. One of them was a short white girl and the other — "No way!"

A horn honked and before Jesse could turn his head back around, a loud bang grounded out as the airbag deployed, hitting him like a punch in the face. The truck jerked forward and then settled back. A combination of blood and gunpowder lingered in the air. Before Jesse could figure out what had happened, the truck jerked forward again as another vehicle plowed into the back of him.

Then again. And again. And again. When finally the world was motionless once again, and the ringing in his ears slowed to a low hum, sirens rang out. He closed his eyes. What a fitting ending to a fantastic day.

"Are you okay, mister?" a woman's voice echoed through his befuddled brain.

Jesse touched his hand to his face, and it came back bloody. "I'm not sure." He opened his eyes and what he saw was a vision, an apparition… an angel? "Maya?"

The angel's warm brown hand raised to her mouth, and her eyes grew wide. "Jesse?"

Before Jesse could answer, his head spun and the next thing he knew, the world had gone foggy on him. The sound of Maya's frantic voice, calling for help streamed through his brain as if he were in heaven, and she was his personal guide.

He could feel the tugging and pulling of his body as hands extricated him from his father's truck. Chances were, the truck had fared much better than any of the other vehicles. Then why was he in so much pain? Nothing made sense.

Jesse tried to open his eyes but found that even more impossible than comprehending the jumble of voices clashing around him.

7

———

MAYA

Frantically, Maya watched as the EMTs strapped Jesse onto the gurney and placed him in the back of the ambulance.

"You better call Mrs. James," Hailey said as she stood beside Maya, rubbing her arms. "She's going to have a heart attack."

"Me?" Maya was still in shock over seeing Jesse, let alone the condition he was in.

"Yeah, you. I can't call. Mrs. J. will ask me what I was doing at the coffee shop in the first place. I'm still on the clock."

"She doesn't own you. You're a taxi driver."

Hailey laughed as though Maya's words were a joke. "Believe me. Mrs. James owns the entire town. It will be better coming from you."

"Okay." Maya let out a huff. "But can you take me back to the apartment first? Benjamin will be home soon."

Maya's entire body shuddered at the sight of Jesse. Mixed emotions whirled inside of her. Under no circumstances was he supposed to know where she was. That was the deal. Benjamin got his every need taken care of as long as Maya kept his identity a secret and stayed away from Jesse if he were ever to come back for any reason. It was all in the contract. Not only could Mrs. James cut Benjamin off, the contract stated clearly that if Maya was to breach it, she would be liable to pay back all funds given to her and Benjamin. That included the hospital and doctor bills, the apartment Mrs. James had lavishly furnished and paid for, the clothes on their bodies and the food that came once a week that filled her cupboard and refrigerator. Everything would be gone.

Bile rose the back of her throat. What had she done? Why had she ran up to that vehicle? There were at least five cars in the collision. Why had she chosen the truck? Why had she gotten involved at all? Maya pulled her phone from her pocket and dialed Mrs. James.

"Hi, Maya. I was just about to call you," Mrs. James answered. "I won't be seeing Benjamin this weekend. We'll work things out soon, though."

"Mrs. James, I uh… it's Jesse."

"Jesse? What about him? He's in with his father right now, and I know I don't have to tell you—"

"Uh… I don't think he's…" Maybe she was wrong. Maybe that wasn't him. Nonsense. She'd know Jesse anywhere. He hadn't changed hardly at all in the last six years. "Are you sure he's with his father?"

"Of course he is. I just left—" Her voice sounded labored as her high heels clicked through the line. "He was right here. Honey,—" Mrs. James' voice muffled, as if she'd covered the phone. "Where is Jesse?"

Muffled arguing sounded as apparently Jesse was not with his father. Maya turned to Hailey and whispered, "They're arguing." She pointed to the phone.

"Who?"

"Mr. and Mrs. James. They—"

"Maya!" Mrs. James came back on the line, her voice distressed. "Where did you see him? You did not break our agreement did you?"

"He was in an accident in Mr. James' truck. It was five vehicles or so. I don't know if he—" Maya looked at Hailey then turned away. She hated to lie, but she had to. "No. I don't think he saw me."

"Are you sure?"

"I was pretty far away. I'm not even sure if it was him, but it looked like him."

Hailey gave Maya a questioning look and Maya pleaded with her for understanding with her eyes. Why hadn't she thought the whole thing through before calling? Of course Mrs. James would have wanted assurances she hadn't contacted Jesse.

"Where is he now?"

"They were putting him in the back of an ambulance. I'm sure he's at the hospital by now."

"Okay, Maya. Go back to your apartment and stay there. I'll let you know what's going on as soon as I get the details."

"Yes, Mrs. James." Maya hung up and stared at the phone. If only she could scream at the woman and tell her how unfair it was that Benjamin's father was right there in the same town, and he couldn't even meet him. Did the color of his skin really matter that much? Benjamin was very light in color and what would it matter if he wasn't, anyway? Mrs. James had no problem taking him on Saturdays. They'd gone to the mall, restaurants, all over the place. Maya never once asked Mrs. James how she'd referred to him. Did she tell people he was just some charity case she'd taken up? Most certainly, she made up some kind of story.

"What are you going to do?" Hailey asked.

"I don't know. Go home, I guess. What else can I do?"

"When Mrs. James finds out Jesse not only saw you, but called out your name, she's going to be—"

"I know. What should I do?" A shiver ran through Maya at the thought that she might have just ruined Benjamin's only chance at a good life.

"Maybe you should go see him before she does? Make him promise not to tell?"

"How? She's got to be on her way there now, and I have Benjamin coming home from school. I'll never make it... Hailey, what if you go?"

"Me?" Hailey looked behind her as if Maya could have possibly been talking to someone else. "Not me. No way."

"Please?" Maya pushed her bottom lip out, hoping she looked desperate, pitiful.

"And tell him what?"

"Just tell him—" Maya hadn't gotten the chance to really come up with an idea. "Tell him simply that he must not mention seeing me. Give him this—" Maya scrounged through her purse, pulled out a folded piece of paper from her son's practice notebook, and scribbled down her number. "Tell him if he wants to know why, he'll have to call me when his mother is not around."

Hailey's shoulders shrunk. "What are you making me do?"

"Please, Hailey. You don't have to say anything. Wait—" Maya ripped off a bigger section of paper and scribbled a message to Jesse. "There. You don't have to say anything. Just hand him this when no one is looking and walk away."

"What if Mrs. James sees me?"

"You're a taxi driver, Hailey. Just say you were dropping someone off."

"In his hospital room?"

Maya gave Hailey a look of desperation. "Please, Hailey. For Benji."

"Fine." Hailey took the folded paper. "For Benji. I better hurry."

"Thank you." Maya hugged her friend. "Thank you so much." Maya got out of the taxi and headed up to her apartment. She turned and watched Hailey drive away, almost wishing she hadn't given her that note.

What would Jesse say? Would it only make matters worse when he read it? For years Maya had told herself that Jesse had not cared about her, that it had only been some kind of crazy prank, but Maya's memory served her differently.

She remembered his warm looks, his playfulness, his pretending he didn't get something just so she would explain it one more time. By the second year of tutoring, Jesse didn't even need her help. She'd told him that many times, but he'd insisted he just was a dumb jock and he was hopeless without her. She'd never laughed so hard as when she was with Jesse. He'd made her glad she'd taken the scholarship to get into a better school. Her mother would have never afforded the school on her own. Maya had worked hard all of her life to get perfect grades. Her mother had told her she would get a scholarship to one of the best schools in the country. Nothing could stop her from being anything she wanted to be. And then Maya's entire world had caved in on her. She hadn't even gotten the chance to tell her mother that she was pregnant before she'd passed away.

Maya went inside and waited for Benjamin. Her nerves were so tightly wound she might burst at any moment. What would Jesse say? What was he thinking? He'd been so out of it when Maya had come up to the truck. His face was bloody, his eyes glossy. He looked as though he'd suffered a concussion. And he seemed more confused than anything, that he was seeing her of all people. Hadn't he known she was still living there?

Maya pulled out her phone and texted Hailey — *Tell me what he says.*

A text came back immediately — *I can't reply right now because I am driving, but I will be sure to get back with you as soon as possible.*

"Oh, Hailey. You are such a good girl." It was an automated response. All taxi drivers for the company had to plug their phones into their vehicles when they drove. Hailey had complained about it on many occasions but it was a safety feature that protected the local cab company from having to pay for too many accidents.

A vehicle honked outside, alerting Maya that Benjamin was home. She went to the window and waved. Benjamin waved back and ran up the sidewalk to the door. Maya hit the button to open it for him and met him in the hallway.

"Hey, buddy!" Maya held her son tight. "How was school?"

"It was okay."

"What did you learn today?"

"I learned that Doyle Anderson is the third. His dad's name is Doyle and his dad's dad too. Isn't that cool? What's my dad's name, Mom? Am I named after him?"

Maya let out an exasperated sigh. It wasn't the first time her son had asked about his father. "I meant school work, Benjamin. What did you learn in school?"

"Oh." Benjamin went inside the apartment and flopped his backpack onto the sofa. "I don't know."

Maya hated to disappoint him. She wanted him to know his father just as much as he wanted to know him. Jesse would have been a great dad. The thought of him interacting with his son made her long to see him. If only…

8
—————

JESSE

Jesse sat on the edge of the hospital bed, waiting to be released. He'd been seen by the doctor and advised that he had a small concussion but that he'd suffered nothing more extensive than that and a few cuts on his face. If that were true, why had he hallucinated seeing Maya? It had to be a figment of his imagination because no sooner was she there - like a poof, she'd disappeared.

Jesse ran a hand through his short yet wayward hair. He didn't want it to be a vision. He wanted it to be real. He'd woken up on the way to the hospital and the first thing he'd asked was to call his mother.

Unfortunately, no one had located his cell phone, but before he'd had time to call her from the hospital, a nurse had come in to tell him she was on the way. Lucky for him, his father was in a different hospital on the other side of town. He wanted nothing to do with the man and the first chance he got he was getting back on a plane and heading to Guam.

The navy had been good to him. It had trained him to do things his parents never had. Like how to be responsible for his actions and how to get up in the morning before the sun. They'd taught him how to iron and fold his own clothes and that he wasn't sick unless they said he was. They showed him that teamwork was an effort that would save lives and that questioning authority could just as easily lose lives.

The navy also gave him a place to lay his head at night and a family that saw him as just another human being. He received no favoritism because of his father. He worked for everything he got. The navy was his home. His family. It was the only place he felt comfortable.

"Eh, hem. Mr. James?"

Jesse looked up. A woman right around his age who looked vaguely familiar stood in the doorway.

"Yes. Can I help you?"

"Sorry to bother you." She stepped forward and Jesse recognized she was the woman coming out of the coffee shop with Maya. "I have a message for you, and then I'll be out of your hair." She drew closer.

"You sure it's for me and not my father? He's in the hospital too, you know."

The girl smiled, her eyes seeming to light with amusement. "I'm positive." She held out a folded slip of paper.

Jesse took it and held it for a moment. "Do you have a name?"

"Hailey. I'm a taxi driver and a friend of—"

"I'll have you know I am his mother!" The strained voice came from the hallway, interrupting them. "I must see him now!"

"Oh!" Hailey pressed closer. "I tried to get them to stall her. I don't think it's working. Read it quickly before she comes in."

Jesse raised an eyebrow at her, and she nodded frantically for him to open it. Jesse opened the paper and his breath caught at what he read.

Jesse, please keep our meeting a secret from your mother. I promise to explain if you call me — Maya. Her number was written below her name.

"I have to go. If your mother sees me speaking—"

"I think I can find his room myself." His mother sounded as if she were right outside his door.

Hailey's eyes bulged, and she shifted like a scared rabbit and glanced at the door.

"Go into the bathroom until she leaves." Jesse waved her inside as his mother entered the room. Folding up the note, he palmed it and placed his hand under the covers.

"Hi, Mom." Jesse touched the small bandage on his forehead. "Nothing to worry about. The doctor says I'm fine."

"That is not what he said!" His mother placed her hands on her hips. "He said you have a concussion. Why in the world were you not there with your father? Jesse, you promised—"

Jesse's hand grew sweaty around the note in his palm. "No, Mom. I didn't promise you anything. I said I would come home but to be honest, it was all just a waste of time." But it wasn't. He'd really seen Maya. She'd been there, and she'd sent the woman in his bathroom to prove it. Jesse glanced at the darkened bathroom. The door was open but Hailey was nowhere to be seen.

"Oh, stop it. You're father isn't himself. He's happy to see you. You just come on back—"

"I'm going home to lie down, Mom."

"But your father—"

"I've got a headache right now. I'm not going back in there to have him treat me like a piece of trash. Not with the way I'm feeling right now."

"Oh, of course." His mother came closer and touched his hand. "You get some sleep. I'll tell your father something. He'll be fine."

"Dad doesn't want to see me, Mom. He made that clear the minute I was in there." Jesse's eyes went back to the bathroom. He needed to call Maya and find out what was going on. "Did anyone happen to recover my phone?"

"Oh, yes!" She dug into her purse and pulled out his phone. "This thing is old. You should really think about updating it."

"Right." Jesse took his phone, grateful that it hadn't seemed to suffer any injury. "If you could get Henry to come pick me up, you can get back to Dad." He glanced at the bathroom door again.

"What's going on, Jesse?" His mother looked at the bathroom door too. "Why are you in such a hurry to get me out of here?"

"No hurry, Mom." Jesse couldn't seem to stop himself from glancing at that door. He looked as guilty as a mouse stuck in a mousetrap, but he couldn't help himself. That woman in the bathroom signified something he didn't dare wish for. Maya had tried to contact him, and he would call her back as soon as his mother left the room.

His mother walked to the bathroom and took a peek inside. "What are you hiding in here, Jesse Carter James?"

"Nothing, Mom." Jesse held his breath while she turned on the light.

"Hailey? What are you doing in here?"

"I... I..."

"I asked her here." Jesse came to the rescue. "We... uh... we're dating." *Dating?*

"You what?" His mother flipped around and stared at him.

Hailey stood in the background, her face flushed.

His mother turned back to Hailey. "Why did you never tell me you were seeing my son? He's been—" She turned back to Jesse. "You've been seeing her long distance? What's going on here?"

"It's no big deal, Mom. It's nothing serious. Hailey and I have been writing back and forth over the years. That's all."

"You... and the... a taxi driver?" She spun back around to the bathroom. "No offense, Hailey." Flipping back to Jesse she said, "Why are you hiding her in the bathroom?"

"We just weren't ready to tell anyone yet." Jesse gave Hailey a wink, feeling the life come back to him. "You know, In case it doesn't work out."

"Well, then. I um... I think maybe we shouldn't mention this to your father... uh, right away?"

"Right." Jesse couldn't agree more. "Good idea."

"Well, then. We'll talk about this all a bit more later. I've got to get back to see your father." She gave Hailey another look, shook her head, and then turned back to Jesse. "You and Hailey? I didn't think you two even knew each other."

"Small world," Hailey choked out, and Jesse almost burst out in laughter.

"Okay, Mom." Jesse gave his mother a light hug. "I've got a couple of errands to run, but I'll be home before you."

"Call Henry," his mother said. "Have him drive you around. We don't need any more accidents, and I think Hailey here is on the clock."

Hailey nodded and backed away. "It was nice seeing you, Jesse. I'll talk to you later." She waved shyly and left before his mother could say another word.

"Well, that was awkward. The bathroom? Really, Jesse? And a taxi driver? You are determined to give your father and I—"

"Save it, Mom. It's nothing serious. Really."

She opened her mouth to no doubt beg to differ that dating a poor, taxi driver was serious business, but then seemed to change her mind. Waving her hand in the air, his mother left the room. Jesse had an idea of what she wanted to say, and he didn't care to hear it. She walked away in silence yet her body language screamed louder than if she'd spoken — *Can't you seem to find a woman of the same caliber?*

As he stood there, waiting for her to leave, he remembered a story his father once told him. Jesse's great-grandfather had been a dirt-poor potato farmer from Michigan. He'd grown up without running water or electricity. His grandfather had left the family farm at sixteen and headed to the city to strike out on his own. His father spoke of the hard life his father had to endure. Of sleeping out in the cold, eating only when he could find or steal something, showering rarely... that was, until one day, his grandfather had discovered he had a useful resource — his brain. Grandpa Leroy had slipped his way into a company, made his way to the top, and eventually, he took over that company. He'd worked hard, slept in the basement, did everything, right or wrong, that he could to make it to the top. He stepped on people, mowed them over, cheated, lied, scammed, but Grandpa Leroy made it to the top.

"And I'll be damned if I let some snot-nosed punk like you bring this corporation to the ground by sneaking around with some..." Those were the last words his father had said to him before he'd shipped him off to boarding school. Jesse hadn't waited to hear that last word, but he could imagine any of the derogatory names that his father had spouted over the years. None of them were nice.

The nurse came in, handed him a prescription for pain medications, and told him to report to his primary care in a week, sooner, if he had any of the following symptoms. She handed him a paper lined with every symptom from memory loss to double vision. As he took it, the small folded paper fell out of his hand.

"Oh." He snapped it up and shoved it into his pocket. Since he'd only been in the emergency room, he was still in his jeans and tee shirt. Listening to the nurse's long spiel about signs to look for and what not to do, Jesse felt his patience waning. Being a Hospital Corpsman in the Navy, he already knew the signs, and he was well aware of what to do and not do.

"Thank you. I'll be sure to check in with my primary care." Smiling, he grabbed his things and left the room. The only thing on his mind was speaking to Maya.

Once outside, Jesse called Henry and asked him to pick him up. The urge to call Maya niggled at him but he pushed it away. For the first time since he'd gotten her note, he had time to think and something wasn't right.

Why had Maya been so adamant about him not telling his mother he'd seen her? His mother hadn't even asked. Why had Maya sent a random woman to the hospital with such an urgent request? And why hadn't she come herself? And what was she doing back in town? There were several more questions clouding Jesse's brain, but he had no time to think about them because before he knew it, Henry had pulled up in front of the hospital.

"Looks like you got hit with a baseball bat," Henry said, rolling down the window. "Shall I get the door for you, or do you think you can manage?"

Jesse opened the back door to the limo and slipped inside. "Do I look that bad?"

"Not too bad, Master Jesse. Just don't look in the mirror anytime soon."

"Henry?"

"Yes, Master Jesse?" Henry pulled out of the parking lot, heading for the James' Mansion.

"Have you seen Maya around?"

"Maya?"

"Maya Brown. You know, she was my tutor back in high school. You used to pick her up on Wednesdays."

"Oh, Maya." Henry threw Jesse a knowing look. "Of course, I've seen her. She works for your father."

"She what?" Jesse's eyes about popped out of their sockets. "She works for… why would my father hire… wait, you mean she works in the household?"

"She's your father's secretary. She has been for some time now."

Nothing made sense. Jesse grabbed his head as a throb pulsed through it.

9
———

MAYA

"What did I do?" Maya chewed the inside of her cheek and paced her bedroom, her eyes wide. "What was I thinking?"

What if he doesn't call? What if he told his mother, and they're on their way right now to throw you and Benjamin on the streets? What will you do then, Ms. Smartypants? Stupid, stupid, stupid! Why would you risk your son's life like this? You have it made! You have everything you need! Benjamin has it made. Why would you do that to him?

Maya dropped to the couch with a shudder. There were a million reasons to never speak to Jesse again. She had everything to lose and nothing to gain by revealing Benjamin to his father. But somehow, in her stupid brain, Maya had thought differently when she'd seen him. She'd thought that they could be together and raise Benjamin as a family. That she would be happy and whole again and Benjamin would be too. He'd never had to suffer a day in his life. He'd had it all. Everything he could ever want and everything he could ever need. But the same thing Benjamin was missing now was what Jesse had missed all of his childhood — the love of a father. Sure, Jesse's father had been there, but he'd never been —

there. He'd never been supportive or loving. For all purposes, Jesse had been raised by his mother. He would want to know that he had a child. He deserved to know. Whether he cared for Maya or not, Benjamin was his son.

A text came in - *Message delivered.*

Maya sighed. It was too late. She couldn't change anything now. Jesse had her number now, and what he did with it was up to him. Maya prayed Benjamin would not suffer for her stupidity.

Maya started to type but instead she called Hailey. Her *Do No Disturb — I'm Driving* bit came on and Maya groaned in frustration.

"Mommy, are you okay?"

Maya looked up to see Benjamin standing in the doorway. "Hey, buddy. Are you finished with your homework?"

"I need your help writing my name. Mrs. Carter says I write my B's backwards. Why does my name have to be so long, anyway? Ava only has three letters in her name."

"Well, mister." Maya patted his head. "I named you after your great-grandfather and he was a great man, just like you. Let's go see what we can do about those backwards Bs."

"I'm not a man yet, Mommy." Benjamin followed his mother out. "Why can't I just write Ben?"

Maya's phone rang just as they left the room. She looked back to see it sitting on her bed. "Go on in the kitchen. I'll be right there. Mommy has to take this call." The thought of it being Jesse gave Maya goosebumps. What if it was him? What would she say? She'd talked herself out of telling him about Benjamin. It was too risky. She just couldn't do it.

Benjamin groaned and left the room. Maya walked on wobbly legs to her bed and lifted her phone in her shaking hand. Her face heated, sweat trickling her neck.

It's just Jesse. Try as she might, that didn't help. The phone rang again and Maya jerked so hard she nearly dropped it. She eyed the screen, the unknown number staring back at her. It had to be him. Well, it didn't have to be. It could be any number of people trying to sell her something, extend insurance on a car she didn't own, or inform her she'd won a million dollars, a flat screen television, and a brand new SUV, but chances were… it was him.

The phone stopped ringing. Just like that. Maya stared down at it. Had she missed his call?

"Moooommmmm!" Benjamin cried. "Do the bumps go in the front or the back?"

"The bumps?" Maya turned toward the door. "What bumps?" She looked back down at her phone. Should she call the number back? But then again, Benjamin's question about bumps seemed concerning.

"The B bumps, Mom! Do they go in the front or the back?"

Her phone beeped, alerting her she had a voice mail. She dropped it as if it were a snake. It clattered to the floor, and Maya stared down at it, unmoving.

"Mo-om!"

"Front, buddy!" she called out to her son, staring at her phone. "The bumps go in front!"

"Okay! Are you coming soon? I'm hungry!"

"Yes, bud. I'll be there in a minute. Mommy has to make a call." Maya leaned down and picked up her phone. Although the last thing she wanted to do was throw Benjamin's life down the drain, she had to at least speak to Jesse. If he had actually told his mother that he knew she was there, and had spoken to her, Maya and Benjamin would be out on the streets faster than she could explain. There were just too many reasons to shut her mouth.

But Jesse, by all rights, was rich himself, wasn't he? He was the heir to billions of dollars. If she told him, maybe he could do… something.

"Mom!"

"Okay, buddy. Give me a second." Maya took one more look at her phone, shoved it in her pocket, then ran out and poured Benjamin a cup of milk. She grabbed some cookies from the pantry and then sat them in front of him. "Don't eat them all. You'll ruin your supper."

Benjamin took a drink of his milk then smiled up at Maya with the most adorable milk mustache. "Okay, Mom. I promise."

"Good boy. Mommy is going to go make my call now."

"Mom?" Benjamin spoke through a mouthful of cookies.

"Yes, son?"

"I'm a big boy now. I'm in Kindergarten. I can't call you Mommy anymore."

Maya pushed out her bottom lip at her little boy. "No?"

"Nope. Jeremiah said only babies call their moms mommy."

"You *are* almost an adult." Maya winked at her son. "I suppose you will be off to college next week, too."

Benjamin giggled and turned back to his paper. "Bumps in front. Bumps in front."

Feeling like that wasn't altogether a pleasant phrase for a kinder-gartner to chant, Maya rolled her eyes and let it go. She had bigger fish to fry at the moment. "I'll be right out to make dinner."

Benjamin nodded as she left. He was too absorbed in his cookies and milk to speak.

Maya went back to her room and closed the door. She pulled her phone out of her pocket and turned it on. The voicemail symbol stood out at the top of her notifications. With a nervous jitter, Maya hit the button and the only message played. The second his voice spoke, her heart beat so fast she swore it would burst from her chest. Just the sound of the familiar warm baritone sent shivers up and down her spine.

Maya held her breath. While she heard his words, she wasn't listening to anything he was saying. She stopped the message and played it again.

"Hi, uh… Maya. This is Jesse. I got this number and a very mysterious message from a girl named… uh… Hailey? Maya, if this is really you, could you please call me back? I… I really need to… just call me back, please." The phone beeped and his voice was gone.

Maya flopped onto her bedroom chair. Her mind spun with so much emotion that she felt faint. That voice… It had haunted her for so long. But she had survived and done what she had to do to make a life for her and Benjamin. If only she hadn't gone up to that truck. Why had she even tried to play the role of concerned citizen?

She'd never just strolled up to an accident and tried to assess the situation. She wasn't a doctor, for goodness sakes. What had possessed her to do that?

Her phone rang again, and Maya stared at the screen. Same number, unknown name. It was him. Before she could talk herself out of it, Maya clicked the answer button.

"Hello?" Her voice sounded foreign to her own ears.

"Maya? Maya, is that you?" He sounded frantic. "Where are you? I want to see you."

Indignation welled up inside her. How dare he pretend to care after all this time? How dare he try to act like he hadn't used her for his own sick pleasure long ago?

"Maya?"

"I can't talk long. I just wanted to make sure you didn't tell your mother that we saw each other, that's all."

"Why?"

"You know why, Jesse." But he didn't. Jesse had no clue the real reason Maya could never see him again.

"Maya, that was a long time ago. We're adults now. I want to see you. I can explain."

"Explain what?" Tears welled in her eyes. "How you used and abused me just because Doyle Anderson dared you to? Do you really think you could explain that away?"

"No. Maya, it wasn't… I mean, yeah. He egged me on, but Maya, I liked you. I mean, I still… please. Can we just go somewhere and talk?"

"And then when your father called me a—" She couldn't dare recite the words, but she needed to. The memory was almost unbearable, but she needed to make him see how hurt she was. "A dirty black whore! You didn't even stand up for me, Jesse. You just let him…" Her throat burned as anger crept up the back. "You just let him call me that. And you…" It would serve no good to rehash the past. "I can't, Jesse. I just wanted you to know that if you tell your mom that you saw me, there will be repercussions for both of us."

"Repercussions? What repercussions? Maya we are not teenagers anymore. My parents don't run my life."

"I have to go, Jesse. Thanks for calling. I trust you will keep our brief meeting quiet. It won't happen again."

"Wait-" Jesse called, but Maya hit the end button, cutting off his words before he could work his charm. She didn't want to hear his excuses. She didn't want to know what he had to say. After all these years, it didn't matter. They were stupid kids, and now, they were adults and Maya had responsibilities.

Now… now they had to live with the consequences of their actions. At least Maya did. Jesse would be none the wiser. He would spend a couple of days visiting with his family and then go back to wherever he'd been for the last six years. For all she knew he had a wife and three children waiting at home - wherever that was.

Her phone beeped with a text message. She stared at it.

"Mommmmm!" Benjamin called, startling her. "I need you again!"

Without reading the message, Maya set her phone down and left the room. The best and only thing she could do was ignore Jesse and hope that he adhered to her warning. Inside, a small piece of her hoped he wouldn't. That little, tiny place in the back of her heart that still beat for him wished he would find out and that he would claim Benjamin as his own so the three of them could be happy together. It was all she ever wished for. But how could she know for sure?

"What's up, buddy?" She leaned over her son from behind.

"Seriously, Mom! Next time you have a kid. Can you *not* give them such a long name?"

"It's a deal." She squeezed his shoulders. "Maybe just a letter? Next kid I'll just name A. How about that?"

Benjamin chuckled. "How about Z? That would be a totally cool name."

"Z it is. Go change your clothes. I'm taking you out for pizza for dinner."

"Yes!" Benjamin made the universal sign of glee by punching a fist in the air and ran from the room.

Besides Mrs. James' provisions, Maya received a paycheck for her position as Mr. James' secretary. That income went directly into a savings account for her future. She couldn't expect Mrs. James to support her after Benjamin was grown. She didn't want the woman to take care of them at all. She'd preferred to do it on her own, but she could never in a million years provide for her son the way Mrs. James did.

The text message flew to the forefront of her mind. What had it said? It was from Jesse, that she was sure of. Not many people ever texted her. Except for Hailey — Oh! Maya got up and ran to her room. What if it was Hailey? By the time she was back in her room, she'd convinced herself that reading the text even if it was from Jesse would do no harm.

Upon entering the room, her phone dinged again. Before she reached her bed, it dinged again. As she picked it up, it dinged again. By the time she opened her screen it dinged another time. Whoever it was, was very persistent.

Ten missed calls and twenty-three text messages awaited Maya on her phone.

The last one said only two words — *Maya, please.*

She scrolled to the top of the text and read. The words on the screen brought tears to her eyes.

"You ready, Mom?" Benjamin stood in her doorway, looking like such a big boy.

"Give me a second, bud. Mommy… uh—" she sniffled. "Mom needs to go potty." Turning so her son could not see her tears, she rushed to the bathroom and washed her face in the sink. The words he'd written came back to her, slapping her in the face.

What am I going to do?

10

JESSE

"Come on, Maya. Answer me." Jesse stared at his cell phone. He'd poured out his heart to her in text. He wanted to speak to her in person. Explain why he hadn't defended her to his father and apologize for not standing up for her. He wanted to tell her how much he'd cared for her, and how he'd thought about her every single day for the last six years. But how could he if she wouldn't answer?

His phone dinged, and Jesse stood. Swiping his hand through his hair, he said a small prayer that it was her. He checked his text messages to see an answer. Only eight words came up, but it was enough — *Meet me at The Coffee Spot at nine.*

Jesse pushed out a breath of air. Sending up a small thanks, he sent a text back — *I'll be there.*

With her short and to the point answer, Jesse was elated. His heart felt light and giddy like he used to feel each time Maya came to his house to tutor him. At first he'd hated it. He felt like a dummy for needing a tutor, but his father would accept nothing but straight As and Jesse's Math grade had fallen to a solid C in the eight grade, making his father furious. It hadn't taken long, though, before Jesse enjoyed Maya's weekly visits. In fact, that very first day before she'd left, a crush had grown in his heart. Each week after that, Jesse had looked forward to her coming.

Jesse scrolled back through the texts he had just sent, reading each one. He hadn't explained to her about his father and why he hadn't stuck up for her. He had been afraid of his father. His only excuse for not standing up for her was his fear. But when he'd seen Maya, rushing to get dressed and then running out of the room almost half-naked and scared out of her wits, Jesse had spoken up to his father. It had been too late. Maya had left, and it hadn't mattered that he'd even tried. With each defense, Weiland James overpowered his son with louder words and harsher ridicule.

Maya would call him a coward when he told her, and she would be right. But he would tell her the truth no matter what. If he were going to win her back, Jesse needed to lay his feelings for her out on the line. He needed to admit his faults, apologize for what he'd done, and beg her for forgiveness.

Grabbing his keys, Jesse headed out the door. "Henry?" he called.

"Yes, Master Jesse?" Henry appeared from out of nowhere as he usually did. He was never too far away when someone needed him.

"Henry, you mind taking me to the mall? I need to get a haircut."

"But, Master Jesse. You don't need to go out in town for that. I'll call Conley and have him come by."

Conley had been Jesse's personal barber since he was a kid. He was a fun man who always had a joke or two to share. "Conley must be a hundred years old by now. Besides, I have to pick up a couple of things."

"Hardly a hundred, Master Jesse." Henry rolled his eyes. "He's younger than me."

"Well, that's not saying much. I wouldn't trust you with a pair of scissors either."

"If you insist." Henry pulled a clump of keys from his pocket. "Your mother has advised me that you will not be escorting yourself anywhere. I will be your driver for the duration of your stay."

"One little fender bender, and I'm cut off for the duration?"

Jesse teased. He had no inclination to drive anywhere. That accident had shaken him up pretty badly and the bruises and scrapes on his face were proof that he didn't need to do any more driving on his own for a while. His face burned with heat when he realized once again why he'd gotten into the accident in the first place. It had been Maya. She and that Hailey girl had come out of a store and as soon as he'd seen her, he'd gotten distracted.

"Yes," Henry said firmly. "Shall we take the limo?"

Henry wasn't one to mince words. He was a good man, fair and just, but he would never go against the words of Jesse's mother or father. He was first and foremost loyal to his employer.

"Limo it is, but maybe you could wait out in the car for me?"

"Of course. You are not a child anymore."

"Good. Let's go." Now that they had that settled, Jesse was ready to go. It was amazing how those few simple words from Maya had turned a horrendous couple of days into something bearable. Even in the form of a text, her words were soothing to his soul.

My Maya.

But she wasn't his anymore. It had been six years since he'd even seen her. Certainly she'd moved on. Maybe she was married. Maybe she had kids. Maybe she was happy.

As Jesse got into the limo, he couldn't think about that. She had agreed to meet with him and that was the best he could have hoped for. To be honest, he hadn't expected to see her at all. He'd planned to come home, deal with his father, spend time with his mother, and then head back to Guam. He still had two years left on his second enlistment, so even if his father had croaked right there in the hospital…

Deciding not to think about his father, Jesse stared at the window, thinking instead about what he would say to Maya.

Before long, Henry pulled up to the front of the mall. "I'll park at the back of the lot. Call me when you are ready to leave."

"Okay. I'll be quick." Jesse got out and headed inside.

On top of getting a haircut, Jesse wanted to pick up something for Maya. He didn't know what, but he didn't want to show up at the coffee shop empty-handed.

Thankfully, the barbershop had no line, so Jesse got in and out quickly. Next, he headed to a trinket shop across the way. Maybe he would find something there for her.

"Jesse James!" a female voice called from ahead just as Jesse saw her. It was too late for him to duck into a store.

"Hey, Tina." He gave a small wave. "What are you doing here?"

"I live here." Her face reddened with obvious anger. Her upper lip trembled. "What are you doing showing your face in this town?"

Jesse put his hands in the air. "Just visiting my dad. He's in the hospital."

Her face softened. "Right. I heard about that. I better go." She turned to leave.

"Tina, wait."

Tina spun back around. "Jesse, just do what you came to do and leave. This town is a lot better off without you."

"Okay." He put his hands up again. "Okay." He wanted to apologize for hurting her in high school, but obviously she didn't want to hear it. Anything he could say to her would be mere empty words, anyway. He'd never cared for Tina as anything more than a friend. His face flushed with the truth of it.

Tina had been a cover. He'd dated her just so that his parents wouldn't find out about his feelings for Maya. That was wrong on so many levels. He shouldn't have treated her that way. As he watched her walk away, Jesse realized he'd hurt many people before he left.

Tina walked off in the direction she'd come from. She stopped in front of a table where a man sat with two little kids. She leaned down and kissed him, then sat across from him. The man looked his way and Jesse realized it was Doyle.

What? Tina and Doyle? Those two seemed the oddest couple on the face of the earth. Doyle looked his way but didn't acknowledge him. He didn't blame him. He'd let him down too. At least they were happy together or seemed to be, anyway.

Jesse followed the scent of candles and strolled into the shop. Maya always loved fresh and flowery scents. Maybe he'd buy her a candle. Before he could get in the door though, a short Asian woman met him halfway.

"Jesse James - is that you?" She spoke fast and with an accent. "I tole you to never step foot in my store again!"

Jesse grinned. He and Doyle had gotten caught stealing candles from her store one time when they thought it would be cool to light them up in the desert while they got loaded on pot and beer. Jesse hadn't touched either since. "Aw, come on, Mrs. Chen. I promise I won't - Wait." He reached into his pocket and pulled out his wallet. Handing her a hundred-dollar bill he said, "Here. For your trouble."

"I don't want your money, Mr. Fancy Pants. I want you out of here. You no grow up. You still bad bad bad. Out!" She pointed to the door.

"But Mrs. Chen!" Jesse put his hands in the air once again. He seemed to do that a lot lately. "I just want to buy a candle."

"You no buy! You steal! You cause me great stress! Out!"

"I'm sorry, Mrs. Chen. Here." Jesse held out the bill again. "This will cover your distress, no?"

"You rich kids tink you can buy anytink. You can't buy me, Mr. Hot Shot. You go away, now."

Jesse gave up and backed out of the shop. "Have a good day, Mrs. Chen." How she had remembered him and an incident that happened when he was in the tenth grade was beyond him. Mrs. Chen had a memory like an elephant. He'd just have to try another place, although he was really set on candles, and Mrs. Chen made the best-smelling candles in town. There was this one that she sold that smelled like chocolate chip cookies. He and Maya used to light that one up every time she came over.

"It stimulates your brain cells," she'd told him.

"You stimulate my brain cells," was always his retort, making her shy away.

I need that candle. Jesse turned back to the store. The name was — The Wax Shop. Plain and simple, but the smells from within were anything but simple. Deciding to try one more time, Jesse sucked in a breath and said a brief prayer. Marching back up to the store, he forced himself to go inside.

"Mrs. Chen," he called again, standing in the doorway. "I want to apologize for trying to steal from you."

Mrs. Chen spun around. "Not interested. You go now."

He did want that candle, but more than that, Jesse needed to make amends for his wild childhood. There were so many people in that town that he owed an apology to. People whose feelings he'd stomped upon because he was rich and his father had thrown down money to stop them from calling the police. Jesse owed a lot of people, and Mrs. Chen was only a start.

"Mrs. Chen?" Jesse tried again. "If you will just give me a moment to explain, and then I will get out of your hair."

"I'm waiting." Mrs. Chen wrapped her arms tightly around her chest. "Go ahead, rich boy. Tell me how sorry you are."

Jesse swallowed. "I was a punk back then, and I had no respect for you or anyone else. I am truly sorry. I don't blame you if you don't forgive me. I just want you to know that I am no longer that kid anymore. I've grown up, joined the military, and I—"

"Military? Jesse James, you join the military? Why you do that? Your father filthy rich! He might even own the military."

Jesse smiled. "It's a long story. I just wanted to come and apologize for any harm I might have caused you."

"You forgiven, Jesse James. You big man to say sorry. I still cannot take that money, though."

"What if I bought a hundred dollar candle?" Jesse grinned happily. Out of all the people he'd harmed in his past, Mrs. Chen was the last person he'd have thought of apologizing to. He hadn't thought about that incident in years.

"You want to buy a hundred dollar candle? We no have a candle for that price. You buy five candle for that price."

"I just want one." He saw the one he wanted and pointed to it. It was brown and cream swirled, decorated with a picture of two chocolate chip cookies on a plate. "That one."

"You want dat one?" Mrs. Chen stared at him for a moment. "Dat one? Your mother must have ten of dat one."

Jesse leaned his head to the side and tried the sympathy card. "It's for a very good friend. I have to apologize to her, too. I just hope she is as forgiving as you are."

"You buy dat one. She will forgive you." Mrs. Chen went over and grabbed the biggest sized candle. She brought it to the counter and Jesse followed her. From behind the counter she pulled out a gift box and placed the candle inside. She then wrapped a velvety tan ribbon around the box and tied it into a bow. "You take her this. She forgive you."

"Thank you, Mrs. Chen." Jesse took the bill out of his pocket and handed it to her as he had promised. "I hope you're right."

"I right. You'll see. You be a good boy now, Jesse James. She forgive you."

Jesse took the box and smiled. "Thank you again, Mrs. Chen. And again, I'm really sorry for any trouble I caused."

"You go on now before I take back my forgiveness." Mrs. Chen shooed him toward the door.

Jesse nodded. "Okay, Mrs. Chen. You have a nice day."

"She no like that one, you come back and see me, Jesse James. I have another one for you tomorrow." She lifted a light purple candle. "Maybe Lavender. She like lavender."

"I think this one will do, but thank you. I'll stop back in before I leave."

Mrs. Chen waved him away, and Jesse couldn't get over the feeling of freeness over her accepting his apology. He felt so light and happy. A feeling he hadn't felt in… ever. Maybe there was something to this forgiveness thing. Jesse laughed. Maybe his father could take a lesson from Mrs. Chen.

11

MAYA

After reading Benjamin a story and tucking him in to bed, Maya stood. "Love you, Buddy."

Benjamin yawned and rolled over. "Love you too, Mommy."

Maya kissed his cheek and smiled. Maybe he wasn't too old to call her Mommy yet. At least not when he was sleepy. Maya watched her son drift off to sleep. He was such a sweet boy. Her heart. Her life. No matter how he came about, Maya didn't regret one second of it.

Her phone vibrated in her pocket, and she pulled it out. Backing out of the room, she checked her messages. Just as she thought, it was from Hailey, and she was right outside the front door.

Maya rushed to the door and opened it. Putting her finger up to her lips, she motioned for Hailey to come inside. "Thank you for not knocking," Maya sighed. "I just got him to sleep. All you have to do is sit here and look beautiful. There's food in the fridge, leftover pizza on the counter, and the remote is there."

Hailey gave Maya a look. "Are you sure you want to do this?"

Maya had contemplated that same question all day. "I'm scared."

"Maybe… you shouldn't, you know, meet him. What if Mrs. James finds out? What will that mean for Benjamin?"

"He could lose everything." Maya waved her hands in the air. "This place, his school tuition, clothing, food… everything. I mean, I have a little saved up, and I'd have to get another job, but this could mean a tremendous change for Benjamin… and me too."

"Lemme ask you one question." Hailey took Maya's arm and led her to the couch. "Do you love Jesse?"

"No… uh, well, I guess I did at one time. But Hailey, that was a long time ago. We were in high school then. How could anyone really know what they want in high school?"

"Do you still think about him?"

Maya nodded. "How can I not? Benjamin looks just like his father. I mean, besides the darker skin, but he even acts like him. He has that goofy way he gives me that cockeyed grin when he's being silly and he even… Oh Hailey, what am I going to do?"

"Do you think he still cares for you?"

Jesse's face popped into Maya's head. He'd always been kind to her, and he'd flirted with her so much they could hardly get any work done. But Jesse was a flirt. It was just in his nature.

"I don't know if he ever did." Although Hailey was close to the same age as Maya, she had not gone to the private school Maya and Jesse had gone to. Very few students were chosen for scholarships at the esteemed high school. Maya, with her good grades and a mother who worked in the cafeteria, had gotten a scholarship. Maya had always thought her color also had something to do with it. There were very few minorities in the school and giving scholarships to the underprivileged must have boosted their ratings.

"Why would he be so desperate to meet you then? He doesn't know about Benji, right?" Hailey always called Benjamin that. Since her son didn't seem to mind, Maya never corrected her.

"No of course he doesn't." Maybe Hailey was right. Why would he want to meet with her if he didn't care? Then again, maybe Jesse James was on a mission to pay his debt to society. Jesse had hurt many people before he left. He'd hurt Tina almost as much as he'd hurt Maya. And then there were all the pranks and stuff he and

Doyle had done over the years. Pretty much no one in the city cared for him, yet being that his father owned them all, no one said anything. Just from doing the man's books, Maya knew that most commercial owners in the town had gained a loan from Mr. James or had gotten some kind of help from the man. Most respected him, but Maya knew the man behind the mask was a cruel and evil person.

"Are you going to tell him?"

"I haven't decided." Maya's heart thumped in her chest at the thought of it. She looked down at her watch. It was eight forty-seven. "I better get over there." Goosebumps rose on her arms. Maybe she should call it off.

"Maya, you're shaking." Hailey touched her arms. "Maybe you shouldn't go."

"I am?" Maya looked down to see that she really was trembling. What was she doing? "It's just chilly in here. I'll be okay."

"It's not cold in here. Maya, are you sure?"

Maya stood. If she didn't get up and go, Hailey would talk her out of it. "I better go. If Benjamin wakes up, just read him a story and he'll go back to sleep. He won't though. He never wakes up after he goes to bed." Grabbing her purse, she hugged Hailey. "Thanks. I won't be long."

The Coffee Spot was just down the street. Although Maya had promised herself to never go back into the place after they denied her a position presumably based on the color of her skin, she really didn't have a choice. It was the only coffee shop within walking distance and her only other choice was a gas station that sported a small pizza shop inside with very little seating.

The night air was chilly for early October. Usually it didn't start really cooling off until the end of the month. A car honked as it passed, and Maya jumped, almost falling off the curb. She picked up her pace. Up ahead, in the coffee shop window, the same woman who had refused to even interview her was still working the register and pouring coffee. Maya stopped short before going inside, but there sitting at a table was Jesse. As soon as he saw her, he stood.

At that moment it was like time stood still. Maya stood, staring through the window at the man she'd been secretly in love with for almost a decade. His face sported bruises and a couple of scrapes, but there was no denying who he was.

His lips edged into a nervous smile, and he waved her inside. Maya took a step forward and reached for the door. Her heart thumped in her chest. Her knees were soft, like gummy worms. Her brain ran a million miles a minute.

One step at a time. If she could just make it in the door, coax her legs to continue to where he sat, she would be okay. At least physically, and that was all she was worried about at the moment. The last thing she wanted was to faint right there in front of that racist barista. Maybe she wasn't racist. Maybe she really had filled the position in the half an hour since she'd emailed Maya to interview.

Why am I thinking about that? Maya didn't care whether the lady was or not. It seemed that her brain was focusing on other matters to keep it from the situation at hand. There, only a few feet away from her, was Jesse Carter James. She drew closer, the distance seeming like a million miles. With every step, she seemed further away.

When finally she reached him, Maya gave him a nervous smile. "Hi."

"Hi." Jesse reached out to touch her but stopped short before actually making contact. "You really are here."

"I really am. I never left."

Jesse gave her a strange look but didn't respond to her statement, instead he said, "I'll get you some coffee first. What would you like?"

Maya gave him a simple order of coffee with cream and sugar and watched as Jesse went up to the counter and ordered for the two of them. Maya sat down with her back facing the wall, her eye on the front door. On the table where Jesse had been sitting was a box distinctly wrapped from — *The Wax Shop* — the candle store in the mall. A feeling of nostalgia washed over Maya. One of her favorite things about the James mansion was the unique scents that came from that very candle store. Chocolate Chip Cookie - Jesse used to light that candle just as they sat down to study. Maya hadn't dared go into that store since.

Maya watched Jesse communicate so easily with the woman behind the counter. No doubt she knew he was the son of the richest man in the state hands down. The woman gushed over Jesse as if he were a movie star. Maya wondered what the woman thought about him having coffee with a black woman.

Stop it!

Not all white people were racist, and maybe the woman had a good reason for rejecting her. Not every act was a racist one. Internalizing her thoughts for the woman was a good way to distract herself from the more serious issue at hand, but Maya had to decide about what she was going to tell Jesse. Her heart wanted to tell him. He deserved to know. But her brain, the logical part, told her it was wrong to upset the balance of Benjamin's life. And on the off chance that Jesse would not welcome his son with open arms, where would that leave them?

Jesse came back to the table, receipt in hand. "She'll bring it out to us."

An awkward silence ensued, and for a moment, Maya stared at the wall while Jesse stared at her.

"You want to talk about it?" Jesse asked, leaning his head in to get her attention. "I know you probably hate me. Half the city does." He looked around. "I'm willing to give you front of the line privileges though." He grinned and touched the boxed gift on the table in front of him. "Well, Mrs. Chen got a jump on you, but I think we're good now."

Maya covered a giggle. "Well, if Mrs. Chen can forgive you—"

"She didn't make it easy on me, and I don't expect you to either. I'm sorry for what I did to you, Maya. I took so much from you. So much that you can never get back. I… there's nothing I can say that will ever make things right between us again." His eyes seemed to search hers. "But I'll do anything to make it up to you."

"Tell me something, Jesse." Maya finally looked at him. "Why did you leave and never come back?"

The barista came over with their drinks and set them down in front of them. "Enjoy." She smiled at both of them. "Anything else I can get for you guys?"

Jesse looked at Maya.

"I'm good." Still burning from her earlier issue with the woman, she refused to look at her.

"We're good. Thank you." Jesse smiled at the petite barista then took a few packets of sugar and opened them. Pouring them into his coffee, he said, "I did come back. You were gone. I looked for you everywhere. My mother told me that your family moved away."

Maya stared at him in shock. "Wait, what?"

"During summer break. My parents sent me off to boarding school after, uh, what happened. That summer before my senior year, I came back, and you were gone."

"Your mom told you that my family moved?"

"Yeah. You didn't?"

"Jesse." Maya shifted in her seat. "I have something to tell you. Bear with me because I am terrified here." Everything inside her screamed for her to shut her big mouth. "I need you to understand what happened after you left."

"Okay." Jesse took a sip of his coffee. "You don't have to be scared, though. We're… friends, right?"

Oh, and so much more. She wanted to spill the beans right there and tell him he was the father of her child, but she had to start from the beginning. It was important for him to see the complete picture before popping out with the words — Jesse, you have a son.

"I guess I should start from the beginning."

Jesse nodded.

"That morning, when your father found us in your guest house was only the beginning of disaster for the both of us." The picture of lying naked and vulnerable next to Jesse when his father walked in came into her head and a shudder ran through her. She took a sip of her coffee to warm herself up.

"I'm really sorry about that, Maya. I should have supported you, defended you. It was all my fault and I let my dad call you names and treat you with disrespect. I have never forgiven myself for that."

"I'm over that part. Really." Maybe she wasn't. It hurt to be treated like she had been some kind of seductress who had trapped the rich, white boy in her web. Still, she went on. "Two months later, my mother passed away. I had no one."

"What? How?"

"She was killed in a home invasion. I went from having a pretty normal life to having nothing in an instant, but still that's not—" The break-in that caused her mother's death had been strange enough as it was, and Maya still hadn't grasped the irony of the situation, but there was nothing she could do about it. Mrs. James finding out when she did had been a lifesaver to Maya. She owed the woman plenty.

"I'm so sorry. Is that why you were not here that summer I came back?"

Maya nodded slowly. "Your mother sent me away."

"What?" Jesse stood, nearly tipping over his coffee. "What do you mean? Why would she do that?"

"Sit down, please." Maya looked around. The shop was nearly empty, but Jesse had gotten the attention of the barista along with an older couple who sat a few tables away.

Jesse ran his hands through his hair as he sat back down. "Why did my mother… what does my mother have to do with this?"

12
____

JESSE

Jesse stared at Maya as she finished her story. How had he not known that his mother would be involved somehow? But it still made no sense.

"After my mother passed away, my only choice was to go into a group home or find my father. Neither option was very attractive. I mean, I hadn't seen my father since I was ten, and a group home?"

"So you went to my mom? I mean, not that I care, but I don't see you doing that."

"No. You're right. I didn't. Around that same time I started getting sick. Throwing up all the time, nausea …"

Maya continued to speak, but Jesse was stuck on those last few words. Jesse wasn't stupid. Two months after they had been together, and she was getting nauseous?

"Jesse? Are you listening?"

"Are you saying what I think you are saying? Maya, were you pregnant?"

Maya nodded her head. "They moved me to a group home, but I was able to stay in the same school. Tina and her friends tormented me for months." Tears welled in her eyes. She blinked, and a tear trickled down her cheek, making Jesse want to reach over and pull her close. Wiping it away, she continued to speak. "They called me a whore. They said I was the reason you had to leave. They pushed me, fought me, talked behind my back, terrorized me… until I could hide my growing stomach no longer."

"I have a child?" Jesse's head whirled. "Maya? I have a child?"

Maya nodded again. "When they found out I was pregnant, word spread like the Black Plague. Every single person in the school knew. People I didn't even know, stopped to stare and point at me. But that didn't last long. Soon, they escorted me to the principal's office and firmly expelled for breaking school policy."

"I'm still not understanding." If she was pregnant, where was his child? Why had his mother never told him he was a father? That Maya was pregnant? That she was being tortured in school, or that her mother had passed away? "Where is my child?"

Maya sniffled again. "Let me finish."

Not wanting to know anything else but where his child was, Jesse bit back his frustration and nodded for her to continue. It would do no good to push her, and after all he'd done to her, he owed it to her to at least listen. Besides, it had been almost six years since that night, a couple more minutes would not change things. Still, his mind wandered to his child. What did he or she look like? If she was warm-skinned like Maya, she would be beautiful. If she had any of Maya's features, they would have to lock her up until she was eighteen. Maya was beautiful in every single way. Sitting across from her at that moment, Jesse could hardly stop himself from reaching out and touching her. But wait, maybe it wasn't a little girl. Maybe he had a son? He was dying to know. Jesse shifted as Maya continued.

"So, that same day they kicked me out of school, your mother showed up at the group home. She pulled me out and the next thing I knew she was shipping me off to a boarding school for pregnant girls. I guess that's where I was when you came back."

"Boarding school for pregnant girls? Is there still such a thing?"

"Who knew? I don't know where she found the place, but it was nice." Maya took a sip of her coffee. "It was also very secluded. A little community of rich girls in all stages of pregnancy."

"Did they treat you well?"

"It was okay. I didn't feel like I fit in, but people were nice."

There was no way Jesse could take all the small-talk until Maya told him the one and only thing he wanted to know. "Maya, what about our child?"

"His name is Benjamin." Maya looked down as she stirred her coffee, watching it swirl. "He's five years old, and he's in kindergarten this year." When Maya looked back up, her eyes shone. "He's the sweetest boy in the world, Jesse. He has your eyes. Your mannerisms. He's a mini you. Always trying to act tough, but really just a big teddy—" Maya stopped as if she'd realized she'd gone too far. "He's sleeping right now. Hailey is watching him at my apartment."

I have a son? Jesse took in a deep breath to stave off the emotions that welled up in his throat. He cleared his throat and spoke again. "I want to see him."

"I don't think that's a good idea, Jesse." Fear shone in her eyes.

"What's going on? Why would everyone keep this from me? I would have come home in a second if I thought…" Being raised by a rough and tough father, Jesse was taught that men didn't cry, but he was having a hard time keeping his emotions in check.

"Your mom. She… there was nothing else I could do, Jesse. What could I do? My mom had just died. My dad, only God knows where he is. And you—" She wiped away another tear. "You just left!"

"I'm sorry, Maya." His heart was crushed. Why hadn't he tried harder to find her? Why had he just assumed she'd moved on? "I just needed to get away. I thought—"

"You thought what? Look, Jesse. I get it. We were teenagers, and you were—"

"Don't say that, Maya." Jesse leaned in. "I would have come home. No matter what. I would have come."

"Well, you didn't, and I had to do what I had to do to keep Benjamin safe."

"What did she do?"

"She took care of us, Jesse. She took care of both Benjamin and me. She made sure we had a place to live, clothes on our backs, food

on our table. She pays our rent, electricity, Benjamin's school —
everything. She even picks him up on Saturdays and takes him on
visits."

"But?" There was a but. There always was with his mother.
Although Jesse loved his mother, she could be manipulative, and he
knew it.

"I had to sign a contract. No one can know that Benjamin is
your son. Not you, not your father, not anyone."

Jesse stood, knocking the chair over behind him. "I'll take care
of this right now!"

"Jesse, please!" Maya stood too, her face twisted

One look in her eyes and Jesse turned to mush. He would do
anything for her. Anything.

"What do you want me to do?"

"Just sit down. Listen to me."

Jesse sat.

Maya took a deep breath and continued, "Remember when I
started tutoring you in the eight grade?"

Jesse gave her a what-does-this-have-to-do-with-anything look.

"You struggled with the order of operations. Remember that?"

Jesse chuckled. "Yes. We argued about that all the time. But
finally I got it."

"This is kind of the same thing. I think if we do this right, we
can make it work. But Jesse, you can't go off half-cocked accusing
everyone of everything. This all happened because two immature
teenagers made a huge mistake. We were wrong, Jesse. We caused
this problem. Not your dad or your mom. This was our fault. Your
mother has done the best she can to keep the peace, and she's been
so good to Benjamin."

"I want to see him." So many emotions rolled through Jesse. He
would fight the world for Maya but she was right. Jesse was in no
position to throw blame around. He had left and not only did
Maya have to take the punishment for them both, she'd had to
make hard decisions in order to ensure her son, their son, was
taken care of.

"I'll take you to see him, but I don't want you to wake him. After that, we need to figure out what to do next. Order of operations, okay?"

"Order of operations." An excitement built in Jesse. He had a son. So much time had been lost, but Benjamin was still young. It wasn't too late for Jesse to be a better father to his son than his father was to him. And there were so many things he needed to tell Maya. God was giving him a second chance. Don't blow it, Jesse. "Wait. What is the order?"

Maya watched him for a moment before answering. "For Benjamin's sake, we need to take things slow. He doesn't need his world turned upside down right now. I don't think he should know who you are yet."

"What? Why?"

"Jesse, your father is lying in a hospital bed, dying. The last thing he needs right now is to be slapped in the face with an illegitimate grandchild."

"He's the reason for all of this!" Jesse stood, this time hitting the table, and spilling his coffee. "If it weren't for him, I would have never left."

"Jesse, calm down." Maya grabbed a napkin and mopped up the spill while sending an apologetic look to the older couple, who now seemed to spend a lot of time pretending they were not listening to their conversation. "Getting angry won't change the situation."

Amazed at her calmness, Jesse sat back down. He'd never had a temper except for with his father. Weiland James was the only person in the world who could rile him up like that. "You don't hate him?"

"I worked for him for the last five years. He's not so bad."

"What do you mean, you worked for him?" Hadn't that been what Henry had told him? Still, it seemed unbelievable to him.

"Your mother got me on as his secretary, and he has no idea who I am."

"Why would she do that?" Jesse lifted his cup and pushed a napkin underneath to sop up the ring of coffee on the table. It was easy to believe that his father didn't recognize Maya from the three years that she tutored him. His father was never home. Or even that morning in the guest house. His anger had been so high that Jesse thought his father would suffer a stroke. It was doubtful his father saw anything past his fury.

"She said he was going to support his grandchild whether he knew it or not. I've been working for him since his secretary quit on him five years ago. He treats me okay."

"Right." Jesse ran a hand through his hair. "As long as you aren't dating his son." The heat rose up his neck again. "He'd rather see me in jail than happy."

"We shouldn't … Jesse, it will do no good to … happy?" Maya looked down at her coffee. "Why would you say that?"

It was too early to tell Maya how he felt about her. He'd lost her once, and he had no desire to lose her again. If he blurted out his feelings right then and there, he just might. Being careful with his words, he tried to speak in generalities. "He's always been that way. Whenever something made me happy, he pushed it away." Okay, so that was not how he'd wanted to say it. So instead, he turned to his other concern. "Maya, I'm in the navy. I have two more years to go before I get honorably discharged."

"That's exactly why we need to tread lightly. If she finds out, you know —"

"I'll support you. We don't have to hide anything."

"Jesse!" Maya drew out his name like she used to when he was being unreasonable and wouldn't listen. "Please. This is not math tutoring. I need you to understand the situation fully."

"Then explain it to me."

"I signed a contract. If your mother finds out I told you, she will take away all support, and I will have to pay back whatever support she's already given me. That means hospital bills, housing, food, everything. And I don't put it past your mother to have an itemized record of every single penny she has spent on us." She pushed her coffee cup to the middle of the table. "Besides, Benjamin likes her. She's the only grandmother he has left. Even if he doesn't know who she is to him, he loves her."

"She can't hold you to—" She could. And if Jesse knew his mother as he thought, she would do anything to keep from tarnishing the James' name. There was only one thing that would change the situation. "When my father dies—"

"Jesse James! Don't you dare say that!"

"What? He's going to die, Maya. He has a tumor on his brain. It's inoperable." It was only a matter of time before his father no longer held control over his family. Jesse awaited that day.

"He's your father." Maya's voice seemed to scold him. "I would give anything to have my father in my life."

"And you don't think my son deserves the same?"

13

———

MAYA

Maya opened her apartment door and slipped inside, pulling Jesse in with her. All the way there, she thought about Jesse's words. He was right. Benjamin deserved to know his dad, and not only that, but Jesse was nothing like his own father. The fact still remained that Maya was under the mercy of Mrs. James. Unless she had enough money to repay the woman for all she'd done, there was no way she could break the contract.

Of course there was the fact that Jesse was heir to the James' fortune. Mrs. James had confirmed that Jesse would take over the business, but he still had two years on his enlistment. Would the navy just let him out? Did he even want to get out and take over for his father? So many unanswered questions swirled around her.

"Oh, hi." Hailey stood from her position on the couch. "I didn't know you were bringing him back here."

"I guess you two have met." Obviously, since she'd sent Hailey to the hospital to give him the message. "He wants to see Benjamin."

"You told him?" Hailey's face turned as white as a ghost. "I thought—"

"I know." Still not sure she'd done the right thing, she glanced at Jesse. "I couldn't keep it from him."

"Okay." Hailey gave her a look as if she was insane. "Your death, not mine."

Jesse chuckled. "Don't hide how you feel about my family, now."

"Oh!" Hailey's face reddened. "No offense. You seem like a nice guy." She looked away as if she didn't really believe her own words. Maya didn't blame her. Hailey had never met Jesse, and she'd had many dealings with the James' family. Although she was only a taxi driver, she'd done many covert jobs for Mrs. James. After all, Mrs. James couldn't be seen sending a limo for Maya every time she needed to go somewhere. Hailey was the perfect standby. Maya could have gotten a vehicle of her own, but every single penny she earned, she saved. There was no reason to think Mrs. James would go back on her word, but in Maya's life, she'd learned that there are no guarantees.

"Oh." Jesse held out the box that had been sitting on the table at the coffee shop. "This is for you."

"For me?" Maya took the box. The moment she had it in her hands, she knew exactly what it was. She smiled as the scent teased her nostrils. "Chocolate chip cookie scented candle?"

Jesse nodded. "It used to be your favorite."

"Still is." Maya opened the box and pulled out the candle. "You must have done a lot of groveling to get this."

"Mrs. Chen had me up against a wall." Jesse chuckled. "But I wore her down with my charm."

"Awkward." Hailey put her hands in the air. "I better get going."

Maya laughed. She could only imagine what Hailey was thinking. "Jesse was a handful when he was a kid. He made a few enemies around town. Mrs. Chen was one of them."

"I bet." Hailey seemed unimpressed. "I better let you two have your time together, or whatever. I'll see you tomorrow, May—"

"Mommy?"

All three of them turned around to see a tired, five-year-old standing in the hallway, wearing spiderman pajamas and rubbing his eyes.

"Benjamin!" Maya ran to her son. This was not supposed to happen. She wasn't ready for them to meet. She'd only planned to allow Jesse to see him — asleep. "It's late, honey. Let's get you back to bed."

"Who's that?" Benjamin asked, pointing to Jesse.

"Hi, Benjamin." Jesse came closer. "You sure are a big boy."

No, no, no! This cannot be happening. Maya went into a panic. There was no way this would turn out good. "Let's get you to bed, little guy."

"What's your name?" Benjamin persisted. Of course he did. Benjamin had never seen a man in their apartment. Not ever. And now, he wakes up to a strange man in his living room? Of course he had questions.

"Hi, little guy." Jesse bent down in front of his son, and Maya held her breath. "My name's James. I'm your mom's friend from High School. It's nice to meet you."

Relieved that Jesse had given Benjamin his last name and had not blurted out that he was the boy's father, she relaxed a little. "We have a couple of things to discuss, and you, little man, you have to get to sleep. You have school in the morning."

"Okay, Mom." Benjamin spent another moment looking at Jesse. "Nice to meet you."

"I'll put him back in bed while you two discuss your uh… business." Hailey took Benjamin's hand. "Let's finish that story."

"I'll come in and tuck you in soon, buddy. Jesse and I are almost done." Why she felt guilty for having a man in her house in front of her son, she didn't know. Even if Jesse was his father, she had no business bringing him there and allowing Benjamin to meet him. Not yet, at least.

Once he was gone, Jesse spoke. "He's so… wow!" Jesse rubbed his face. "I can't believe I have a son."

"Shhh." Maya placed a finger over his lips, feeling instantly warmed. "Please." Worry set in so hard that Maya's throat constricted. What she was doing could be dangerous to all of them. Not just for her and Benjamin, but if Mr. James found out, what would he do? Would he disinherit Jesse? Throw him out of the will?

Jesse lowered his voice. "What are we going to do? I want him to know who I am."

"Thank you for not telling him yet. We really need to wait and figure this all out." Although with the current look on his face, Jesse was unpredictable.

"But he's my son." Jesse's voice was almost unheard. "He has to know."

"You better go now." Maya couldn't trust Jesse to not run into Benjamin's room and blurt out the truth. Not only that, but every second she was in the same room with him, emotions overwhelmed her. Reminding herself that he had never had feelings for her like she had for him, she pushed him to the door. "We'll talk more about it later."

"But—"

"No buts. It's late. We'll talk about it tomorrow. You have my number."

Jesse opened his mouth to object, but then closed it again. He walked to the door. "I'll text you."

Maya nodded and watched him leave.

Within seconds, her phone beeped.

14

JESSE

After spending almost the entire night texting with Maya, Jesse was exhausted when his mother called him the next morning. Maya had made him promise he would not say a thing about what he knew to his mother, and although he'd prefer to get it all out in the open, he wasn't sure how his mother would react. She'd done so many things throughout Jesse's life to appease his father, that Jesse wasn't entirely sure she would be sensible about this one topic.

"Hi, Mom," he answered the phone with a yawn. "How's Dad doing?" Not that he cared, but that was why he'd come home.

"Jesse, I need you to get an early release from the military. Now, I've called my lawyer, and he says you can get an honorable discharge for 'unique circumstances.' I've already had him contact your command."

"You what? Mom, you can't just go around running my life anymore." He sat on the edge of his bed. It seemed his mother was controlling more than just his life. She had her hands on several lives. "What if I don't want to get out?"

"Who's going to take over your father's business? It has to be you, and you will need training. If you hadn't been off running the gamut, you would already be ready to take the position."

"I never said I wanted to take over the company, Mom. Besides, I'm sure Dad has made other arrangements. Maybe there's an illegitimate child somewhere who can take over for him?"

"Jesse Carter James! I will not have you bad-mouthing your father like that! He may not have been the best father, but he never stepped out on me!"

Jesse breathed a heavy sigh. "Right. I'm sorry, Mom. I'm just… I don't know—" Then it hit him. Taking over for his father would be the perfect way to control the current situation. If the company were handed down to him, there was no way his mother could hold that contract against Maya. He could tear it up himself. And most of all, he'd be free to tell Maya how he really felt. And maybe, just maybe, he, Maya, and Benjamin could be a family.

"Jesse, please don't fight this. Your father… he's just never been good at expressing himself. He's going to need you in the next couple of months. He needs to know that when he goes, the company will be in excellent hands."

"And he thinks my hands are good?" Just when he'd decided to do whatever he could to take care of Maya, the mere mention of his father's name got him ready to pack his bags and head back to Guam.

"He wants to speak with you. Do you think you could be civil to him? He's dying, Jesse."

Wanting to protest that he was not the one who always started the arguments, Jesse remained quiet. Nothing good would come from laying blame. "Fine. Let me get into the shower, and I'll come up to see him."

"Thank you, Jesse."

Jesse disconnected the call and leaned back on his bed. How had things gotten so difficult so quickly? Only a few days before, he'd been living on an island, hanging out with his buddies, and working at the local hospital. With one trip to the command master chief, Jesse's life had turned upside down. A picture of little Benjamin came to mind, and he smiled. Benjamin and Maya were the silver linings. If he had them by his side, he could endure anything.

"Order of operations, man." Jesse thought about how Maya had tried to get that point through his thick skull when he was a teenager. He'd argued with her so much on that one point it had become a standing joke between them. But that one point was the epitome of his life. Until he'd joined the military, Jesse had had no order in his life at all. He'd done what he wanted, when he wanted, and how he'd wanted. The military had dictated some of his life, but even then, he'd made his own decisions without having to worry about disappointing his father. That was all about to end. Maya and Benjamin needed him. The thought of them brought chills to him that was quickly squashed when he realized he was about to go see his father.

"Might as well get it over with." Jesse stood and proceeded to get ready.

AN HOUR LATER, Jesse stood in the hospital room across from his father. The man looked years older than he had only a day before when he'd seen him. His hair was completely gray, his face pale and almost sunken in, and his eyes seemed to look but not see.

"Hey, Dad." Jesse drew closer. "How you feeling?"

His father's eyes squinted as he focused on his son's face. Realizing who it was, he opened his mouth weakly. "Get out!" Lifting a hand barely off the bed, his father pointed to the door. "I don't want you here!"

"Now, Weiland," Jesse's mother intervened. "You said you wanted to see him, remember?"

His father moved his head around to focus on his mother. "I said no such thing! Get him out of here!" Although there was tension in his voice, the words were stilted.

"Weiland! Jesse is your—"

"It's okay, Mom." Jesse stepped back. "I'm good." Before his mother could say another word, Jesse bolted. Anger fueled his legs as he stormed to the emergency fire exit and took the stairs two at a time. He was done trying. That was it. Jesse didn't care if his father begged him to come back and speak to him. He would never speak to that man again.

His phone rang in his pocket. Jesse pulled it out and checked the screen as he reached the bottom floor. It was his mother. Ignoring the call, he shoved his phone back into his pocket and leaned against the wall. Emotions socked him in the gut, incapacitating him. Sliding to the ground, Jesse dropped his head into his knees and closed his eyes. Staving off tears of years of rejection, Jesse took in a deep breath. His phone rang again, and he pulled it out to silence it.

But it wasn't his mother, it was Maya. Why was it that no matter the circumstances, Maya could elicit joy in his heart? "Hello?"

"Hey. I was just wondering if you wanted to meet for lunch? You know, to talk about our situation?"

"Of course. Where should we meet?"

"My side of town. I don't want to chance anyone seeing us."

At the moment, Jesse harbored so much hate for his parents that he didn't care who knew, but he wouldn't argue. He'd do whatever it took to see her again. They agreed on a meeting place at a quiet little restaurant within walking distance of Maya's apartment, and Jesse had Henry drop him off at a car rental place. He needed to get around without his mother knowing his whereabouts, and he wasn't about to take another one of his father's vehicles out.

Once he rented a decent compact, he headed to the restaurant. Before he could park, he saw her sweet face, staring aimlessly out the window. Her brows were knit, and she looked to be deep in thought. What was she thinking about? Then she saw him, and her countenance changed. Her face lit up like the sun, and she waved at him.

He waved back and went inside. He couldn't help thinking he had missed an enormous opportunity when he'd left. So many things had happened. Things he never could have imagined. He had a son. Jesse James had a son. Now all he had to do was figure out how to be in the boy's life without creating an even bigger mess than he'd already made.

"Hey." Jesse sat across from Maya.

"Hey, yourself." Maya smiled that brilliant smile that always made him tingle down to his toes.

"How's Benjamin doing?"

"He's good." Maya seemed to search his eyes. "I want to tell him, Jesse. I want him to know you."

Jesse leaned in and placed a hand on top of hers. "We will figure this out. I promise."

MAYA

"Tell me what you've been up to all these years," Maya said as soon as the server left with their orders. "I never pegged you for a military man."

Jesse seemed to be somewhere else for a moment, and then he looked at her. "I don't know. You know, it's like I just wanted to get away from all the drama." His eyebrows scrunched up. "And it seems like as soon as I stepped foot back into town it all started back up again. My life has been so simple since I've been gone."

Trying not to be offended by his words, Maya smiled. "What's going on? I know finding out you have a child is pretty overwhelming, but—"

"No." Jesse took her hand again, making her heart pulse. "No. It's not that at all. Finding out I have a son is the best thing that has ever happened to me. I just hate that I have missed so much of his life already."

Maya tried to respond, but the lump caught in the middle of her throat refused to allow any words to pass.

"I wish we didn't have to hide it from everyone else," he continued. "Especially from him. Maya, you cannot believe how much restraint it took to not grab that little guy up and hold him tight and tell him how sorry I am for not being in the first five years of his life. I've missed so much." His eyes glossed, and he looked away. "It's not that at all, believe me."

"Then what is it?"

"What do you think?"

"Your dad."

Jesse looked away.

For as long as Maya had known him, Jesse had been vying for his father's attention. Other people thought Jesse was just a trouble-maker in high school, but Maya knew the truth. He'd done all those things to gain his father's attention, and none of them had succeeded in doing anything but gaining his father's ire. Jesse still looked like a lost child, wishing for his father's affection.

"I just don't get it. Why does he hate me so much?" Grabbing the napkin from in front of him, he rolled out the silverware and began tearing tiny slits into it. "I'm not trying to sound like a martyr. I get it. But why—"

Maya placed her hand over his to stop him from ripping the napkin to shreds. If only she knew the right words to say. The words that would make everything all better for all of them. Instead, she said, "It's not your fault, Jesse."

The server came with their food, and they ate in silence. Being with Jesse again was surreal. If only she could say the words that would fix everything. But the issue before them seemed insur-mountable.

"Maybe we could move to an island somewhere?" Maya joked, but in all reality, it wasn't the worst idea.

"I already live on an island. If you marry me, you can come back with me."

Maya fumbled with her fork, dropping it into her salad. "Jesse —" Confused about the sincerity of his words, she tried to make light of it. "You're so silly."

"I'm serious." Jesse picked up the check on the edge of the table and slid out of the booth. "Let's take a walk. I want to talk to you."

Maya swallowed back the anticipation that edged up the back of her throat. Don't think too much into it. Benjamin is his son, and of course he would want to do what he could to be a father to him — but marriage? As much as she wanted to believe he had once cared for her, she couldn't allow herself to entertain any such fantasies. She followed him out of the restaurant, checking her phone for the time as she went. There was still another two hours before Benjamin was due to arrive home from school.

Once outside, Jesse took her hand in his. The air was a little chilly but the warmth of his hand thawed her entire body. Sadness ran through Maya, filling her emotional bucket to the point of over-flowing. Without warning, her legs went weak and her body shook all over.

"Are you okay?" Jesse pulled Maya to him just as her legs gave way.

Lifting her in the air as if she weighed no more than a penny, Jesse walked over to a bench at the edge of the park. Embarrassed to be carried like a child, Maya wriggled. "I'm okay. Let me down."

"Not until I get you to a place where you can sit down." He pulled her closer and Maya buried her head in his chest. The smell of his cologne put her over the edge again. She shuddered at his touch. How would she ever manage a relationship with him? He was rich, white, and... rich. There was no reason to pursue something with him. And yet, it was the only thing she wanted.

Jesse set her down onto the bench and scooted in next to her, pulling her close. He leaned his head on top of hers and buried his nose in her hair. Rubbing across her back, he asked, "What just happened?"

Maya lifted her head to get a look at him. "I don't know. I got light-headed. That hasn't happened since—" Maya tilted her head back down. It hadn't happened since the day his father had found them together six years before. That day, Maya had been so scared, so alone. And Jesse had left her to fend for herself as he and his father got into a shouting match. That morning, she'd walked three miles to her home in her prom dress and heels. Jesse had never come to see her home safely. "It doesn't matter. Jesse, I should get back to my apartment. Benjamin will be home soon." He hadn't cared for her then. What made her think he cared for her now?

"Maya, please." He pulled up his sleeve and checked his watch. "There's still plenty of time before Benjamin gets home. We need to talk."

They did need to talk. They needed to sort out what was going on between them. As much as she wanted to avoid the truth, she needed to be strong. For Benjamin. He deserved it. Still, Maya looked away.

Jesse placed his hand under her chin and tilted her head so they were nose to nose. "Maya, there's something I need to tell you."

"What?" Her voice had all but disappeared as she gazed into his eyes.

"Maya, I'm sorry. I'm sorry for everything." He took her hands in his. "I was so stupid, so angry. That night, Maya, I —" Jesse stared out into the park where a dog and his owner were playing a game of fetch.

"It's okay. You don't have to apologize. I knew what I was doing."

"No." Jesse brought his attention back to her. "No. Maya. I… I just left you there. My father had made me so angry. We fought for twenty minutes before I realized… I ran back to find you and—"

"You didn't expect me to stay there and wait on your family's property while you argued with your father, did you?"

"I thought… I mean, I guess… Maya, that morning has haunted me for years. I hurt you so badly, and I couldn't even tell you how sorry I was. My father gave me a half an hour to pack my bags before sending me off to boarding school in Indiana."

Maya searched his words for something, anything that said Jesse had felt the same way for her as she felt for him. But it wasn't there. She believed he'd been upset for hurting her. They had built a friendship and no matter how racist his father was, he couldn't take that away from them. But Maya had loved Jesse. As young as she'd been, she'd felt the same then as she did the first time she'd recognized him in the accident. Although the years had dulled her heartbreak, each time she looked into her son's eyes, she yearned to see Jesse again. And now… here he was, and things weren't going at all as she'd dreamed a million times before.

"It's okay. I get it." She didn't, though. She wanted so much more from him, but Maya wasn't about to beg for it.

"I don't think you do." Jesse pulled her closer, kissing her lightly on the cheek. "Maya, I love you. I know it's a lot to take in right now, but I—"

"I love you too." The words gushed out without restraint. No matter how she'd promised she wouldn't go there, she wouldn't make him feel like he was trapped because he had a son with her. In her wildest imagination, she'd never said those four words to him.

"You do?" Jesse lifted her chin again. "You love me? I mean, really love me? How could you? After all I did to you?"

"What did you do?"

"I… Well, I… Apparently, I impregnated you and left you to deal with the consequences alone. Maya, I'm so sorry."

"What are we going to do?"

Jesse pulled her closer. "We'll figure it out." Jesse leaned into her and before she could stop him, not that she would have, his lips covered hers in a deep, all-consuming kiss. When finally he pulled back, he touched her face. "I will make it up to you and Benjamin. I promise."

Maya nodded, ignoring the growing knot in her stomach. Words were easy. That night he'd told her he loved her. He'd kissed her passionately. He'd made love to her. And although everything about the situation had been wrong, it had felt as if they had been made for each other. Nothing had mattered at that moment. Not their skin color, not his bigot father, or her equally racist mother who told her she could never be good enough for Jesse. The only thing Maya had regretted was that she'd broken her own rule. She'd promised to remain pure until her marriage night, and she hadn't. But how could she really regret that? Benjamin was such a joy. She couldn't imagine what life might have been like if she didn't have him.

They stayed together for a long time before Maya realized it was almost time for Benjamin to arrive home. While she wanted to stay with Jesse forever, she sat up with a sigh.

"What are we going to do?"

"Guam?" Jesse raised his eyebrows in that corny way he used to do when she'd asked him a question he couldn't answer.

"Uh, no."

"No?" Jesse pushed out his bottom lip. "Okay. Don't worry. Everything will work out. Just give me some time to speak to my mom about it."

"What?" Maya stood so quickly she almost lost her balance and fell. "No! You can't say a word to her!"

"Maya!" Jesse stood and grabbed her arm to steady her.

"I have to go get Benjamin." Maya pulled away from him. "Don't you dare tell your mother. Not until…" Ever! There was no way they could ever tell Mrs. James. She would make them pay. And most of all, Benjamin would pay.

"Okay. I won't say anything right now." He pulled her closer, and she relented. "But we will have to soon. I don't want to miss any more time in my son's life."

"Just give me time to figure out what to do." A shiver ran through her.

"No way, Maya." Jesse pulled her comfortably close. "Not this time. This time we figure out what to do together."

Maya nodded as words would not get past the lump in her throat. The thought of anything going right between them had seemed so far away until that moment. Maybe they could make it work?

16

———

JESSE

Jesse drove Maya back to her apartment and then sat outside in his rental, waiting for the limo to bring Benjamin home. He wouldn't try to speak to him, but he needed to see him again. He just needed to figure out how to go about everything without making it hard on Maya and Benjamin. He needed a plan, and it had to be a good one.

There was no way Maya would go for him walking into his mother's home and confronting her with what he knew. The old Jesse James would have already had that conversation. He'd have gone off the handle, cursed out both his mother and his father, accused his father of being a bigot and his mother of extortion. He'd have gotten Maya and Benjamin in a huge predicament, and alienated himself from everyone all over again.

Jesse was not a billionaire. His father was. His mother was. But Jesse was just as broke as anyone else serving next to him in the military. His father was the old-fashioned kind who didn't believe a man should get a single dime he hadn't paid for, and Jesse didn't want his father's money.

The limo pulled up, and Jesse's pulse quickened. A minute later, Benjamin exited the car, pulling his backpack up around his shoulders. He looked so handsome in his private school navy-blue uniform. He was such a handsome little guy with his warm brown skin, dark eyes, and those soft curly locks that seemed to fall into his face each time he moved his head.

Jesse placed his hand on his car door to open it just as the door to the apartment building opened.

"Hey, buddy!" Maya ran out to meet her son. "How was school?"

What was he thinking? Jesse hit the auto locks on the door. Obviously, he couldn't control himself around Benjamin. Something needed to happen quickly. He'd lost too much time with both of them.

Jesse's phone rang, making him just about jump out of his skin. He glanced at the screen. It was his mother. He watched Maya guide Benjamin to the door before answering. Just before they disappeared inside, Maya turned around and gave him a warning look. Jesse grinned. Maya couldn't be mean if she tried. It was one of the things he'd loved about her. There was nothing fake about her. She wore her heart on her sleeve, and she made no pretenses about her feelings, whether good or bad.

His phone stopped ringing and before he could pick it up to call his mother back, it started ringing again. It was his mother again.

He answered, "Hey, Mom. Sorry. I was just about to call you back."

"Where are you?" Her voice sounded tired.

"I'm on my way to the hospital now. How's Dad doing?" Somehow, he needed to make amends with his father. Not only would it solve all of their problems, but Jesse tired of the stress between them.

"I'm scared, Jesse. I don't think he has much longer."

"I'm on my way." Jesse pulled out onto the street. "I'll be there in about twenty minutes."

Making record time, Jesse pulled into the hospital parking lot in fifteen. He parked and before he could make it to the main lobby, someone called him from behind. Jesse looked back to see his mother waving at him from behind a large cement pillar.

"Why are you hiding?" Jesse headed toward her. Before he got too close, he could smell the reason why. In her hand was a half-smoked cigarette. "Are you serious, Mom? You quit that habit like ten years ago."

"I never quit." She took a long drag of her cigarette and pulled the smoke deep into her lungs. "I just hid it from you and your father."

Jesse sighed. At the moment, he didn't have the energy to chastise his mother. She was going through too much at the moment. "What's going on with Dad?"

"He's been talking nonsense." Her eyes glistened with unshed tears. "He didn't even recognize me when I went in to see him."

"What did the doctor say?"

"He doesn't have much time left. Jesse, please. Tell him you forgive him."

"Forgive him? Mom, Dad doesn't think he's done anything wrong."

"You father is prideful, but he's not stupid. He knows what he did all those years ago was wrong. He just… Jesse, it's just how your father grew up. It's not that he's … he just worries about you. He wants only the best for you."

"And Maya was not the best thing for me? Why? Because her skin is darker than ours?" Jesse bit his lip at the thought of Benjamin. He was so perfect in every way. "How was sending me away the best thing for me? And where is Maya now, Mom?" He didn't want to deceive her, but he wanted her to come clean. Just maybe the issue could work itself out if she did. His mother was tricky like that. Jesse could only get her to agree to certain things if she thought they were her idea.

His mother took a long drag of her cigarette, butted it out on the sidewalk, and then placed the butt in the front pocket of her purse. "I don't know where she is. She left shortly after you and never returned."

So much for that. "She left, or you sent her away?"

"Can we discuss this when your father is not up there dying?" She looked up at the hospital.

Jesse refused to answer, wishing he could blurt out the truth.

"Please?"

"Yeah. Okay. Let's go see Dad, but it's really a waste of time. I've tried twice, and he doesn't want to see me."

"Oh, stop being so dramatic, Jesse." His mother walked to the end of the parking garage, pulled the butt out of her purse and dropped it into the large cement ashtray. She took a small bottle of perfume from her purse and sprayed herself. She then popped a breath mint into her mouth and squeezed out a dollop of hand sanitizer onto her hands from another bottle from her purse. "Are we ready?"

No wonder his father didn't know she was smoking again. By the time she was done there was no hint of smoke anywhere for at least a block.

Jesse followed his mother back into the building, up the elevator, and into his father's room. With each step, he resolved to be the bigger man. Whatever it took to mend the bridges between him and his father, is what he wanted to do.

Although he'd never admit it out loud, Jesse was no different from his father when it came to pride. Maybe that was why they had butted heads at every turn. Neither of them would ever admit they were wrong. But the stakes had been raised. Jesse didn't care about one-upping his father. He cared about the woman who had captured his heart long ago and the little boy who needed a father. For them, Jesse was willing to set his pride aside.

"Will, how are you feeling, honey?" His mother moved closer to the bed. "I brought Jesse with me. Wouldn't you like to speak to him?"

Jesse closed his eyes as his father glanced around his wife to see him. Silence ensued for a moment before Jesse opened his eyes and took in his father's aging face. To his surprise, this time his father had an expression of confusion instead of anger.

"Jesse?" The stress in the air was so thick that Jesse could hardly breathe.

"Hey, Dad."

"Jesse?" His father's eyes glossed. "My Jesse?"

Jesse shuffled awkwardly. "How you feeling, Dad?"

As if a switch had turned on in his father's head, his demeanor changed instantly. "What are you doing here? I thought I told you I never wanted to see you again!" Spittle flew from his father's mouth as he stared daggers at his son. Then he turned to his wife. "Why won't you let me die in peace?"

Before either of them could respond, the doctor came in, seemingly diffusing the situation. "Mr. James. How are you feeling today?"

"Like a dying man." His father turned his head to the window. "Why won't you just let me die in peace?"

"Yeah." Jesse took a deep breath. "You want peace, you got it." He turned and stormed out of the room.

But as his feet hit the hallway, his father spoke, stopping Jesse in his tracks. "When are you going to tell him he's not even my son?"

17

———

MAYA

Benjamin sat at the small dining room nook and took out his pad of writing paper. Maya had no idea kindergarten would be so much work on her son. Not that she remembered all that much about kindergarten, but she was pretty sure she didn't have three to five pages of homework every day at that young age.

Not that she was complaining. Mrs. James had paid to send Benjamin to the same private school Jesse had gone to as a boy. It was the best in the state, and Benjamin was lucky to have the opportunity. At the rate things were going, Maya wasn't sure what would happen next.

Mrs. James seemed to know things. It hadn't taken long at all for her to find out that Maya was carrying her grandson. Soon after Maya's mother died, Mrs. James had spared no time in taking control of the situation. It was what she did. She was a problem solver. Only this time, it would not be so easy to sweep the truth under a proverbial rug.

"Mom?" Benjamin looked up from his paper. "Who is that guy, anyway?"

"What guy?" Maya pretended she didn't know what he was talking about.

"You know. That guy who was here when I woke up. He was in that black car when I got home today." Benjamin went to the window and looked out. "And I heard you talking to him on the phone last night."

Benjamin had taken after Maya in the perception department. Few things got past him. Yet she wasn't ready to come forth with the whole truth. "He's a friend from Mommy's past, buddy. We went to high school together."

"You did?" Benjamin's eyes grew big. "Did he know my dad?"

"Now, why would you ask me something silly like that?" Maya turned away so that her son could not see the truth in her eyes.

"Well, did he?" Benjamin set his pencil on the table and stared at his mother, forcing her to make eye contact.

"I'm not sure how to answer that, buddy." How could she tell her son that he was dipping into a dangerous topic? He was only a boy. How could she place such a burden on him?

"Just tell me, Mom. I'm not a baby anymore."

"No, sweetie, you're not. You are a big, brave boy." Maya struggled to fight back the tears. "And you deserve to know the truth. Could you just give me a little bit of time to figure everything out?"

"I knew it!" Benjamin jumped to his feet and high-fived the air. "He's my dad! I knew he was my dad!"

"Whoa, buddy!" Maya stood, staring in awe at her son. "What… where…" Could she lie to him? Could she really look into his eyes and crush his soul with a dirty lie?

"Cuz, Mom! You get all weird and funny when he's around… Mom, why won't you just tell me?"

Tears burned Maya's eyes, and she turned away from her son. She was a horrible mother to keep the truth from him. No matter how many times she told herself she was doing right by her son, the guilt sucked the life out of her each time she lied to her son. Yet the thought of the truth was also too much to bear.

Benjamin was smart. Just like his momma, he'd always been wise for his age. When Benjamin had hit the nail on the head, she had to make a choice on how to proceed.

"Give me some time to sort this all out, okay?"

"I knew it. He's my Dad! Why didn't you tell me?"

"Wait now. I didn't say—"

"He said his name was James, Mom! Besides, if he wasn't my dad, you would just say so."

He had a point. Maya winced. He was way too smart for his own good. Maybe she should have thought twice about putting him in such an advanced curriculum at such a young age.

Who was she kidding? Benjamin was a spitting image of his father, who looked just like his mother. And neither of them much resembled Mr. James at all.

When Maya's phone rang, she held in a sigh of relief. It gave her the break she needed to figure out what to say next. Pulling it from her purse, she stared at the name that popped onto her screen — Jesse James.

Benjamin, who had started reading at the beginning of the school year, sounded out the words enough to realize who was calling. Grinning, he picked back up his pencil and opened his writing pad. "Tell him I said hi."

Maya may have rolled her eyes, but inside she was shaking. How had everything fallen apart so quickly?

"I'll be right back, buddy." Although Benjamin all but knew the truth, Maya couldn't trust herself to confirm his suspicions until she talked to Jesse.

Answering, Maya stepped into her bedroom and closed the door.

"He's not my dad." Jesse's voice was stilted.

"What? What do you mean? Who's not…"

"Weiland. He's not my father."

"What? Jesse, what are you talking about?"

Jesse let out a deep sigh. "I need to see you."

"Now's not a good time." Maya lowered her voice. "Benjamin knows."

"He knows? What do you mean, he knows? You told him?"

"No!" Maya looked toward the door. "I didn't tell him. He guessed."

"How does a five-year-old guess that kind of thing? Are you sure?"

"Wait, — Jesse. He's not your father? How..." This changed everything. If Weiland James was not Jesse's father, Jesse was not entitled to a single cent of his money. Not that money meant everything, but Maya was in for thousands of dollars to the James' family. She'd felt somewhat comforted that Jesse was receptive to being a father. With him there, together or not, he would take care of his son. If nothing else, they could fight together. But now, if what he was saying was true, then Jesse had no more power than she did.

His statement opened a whole can of worms that Maya would have never expected. "What are you going to do?"

"I need to see you. Can I come by?"

"But Benjamin—"

"You said he knows."

"He doesn't know, Jesse. He just thinks he knows."

"Then we'll tell him." The phone disconnected before Maya could argue.

Maya stared at the phone for a long while before she decided she should prepare her son for what was to come. Trying to wrap her mind around that one fact was like trying to rip off a bandage so fast that it burned the skin. Only this was no bandage. If Jesse was not a real James', Maya and Benjamin's only hope for the future was about to blow up in her face.

"Hey, buddy. Are you finished with your homework?" Maya reached for the blue homework folder that Benjamin was shoving back into his backpack. "Let's see your work."

Benjamin pulled it from her and shoved it back into his backpack. "I'm done, Mom. You don't have to check it every time."

"Of course I do." Maya tried once more to retrieve the folder her son was clinging to his chest. "Benjamin, let go. What's wrong with you?"

Benjamin finally released the folder and slumped back in his seat. "Fine. But it's all your fault."

"What's my fault?" Maya opened the folder. His pages were neatly placed in the completed side, his name written on the top and his B-bumps facing front. She inspected his work. His printing was perfect as usual. "You did a great job, Benjamin. Why were you trying to hide it from me?"

Benjamin took the pencil from in front of him and handed it to Maya. "Good. Then can you just sign my agenda?"

"Sign your agenda?" There was only one reason they required a parent to sign their student's agenda. "Benjamin?" She flipped to the front. "Why are you on red? You always get at least green." He'd been on purple the entire week, which was the best 'color' a kid could get.

Benjamin lowered his head as Maya read the comments in his agenda — Benjamin was acting quite out of character today — shoving, pushing, fighting.

"Benjamin? You got into a fight at school?" Maya stared down at her son, eyes wide in astonishment. She sat down next to him. "What happened?"

"Doyle called me a leech. He said you are one and I am, too. He said I don't belong there, and his mom told him he can't be my friend anymore."

"A leech? What does that mean?"

"How am I supposed to know?" Benjamin turned away, anger lighting his young eyes.

"Benjamin? What did you do when he said that?"

"I socked him in the gut!" Benjamin balled his hands into fists. His face hardened, showing a toughness Maya had never seen before.

Maya counted to five and breathed in. The last thing she wanted was for Benjamin to have to grow up tough like she did.

Tina. In her mind, she could still see the woman as a vengeful teen, yet now as a grown adult, she still hadn't gotten over that night. Maybe no one had. That night had changed so many things for all of them.

That night, after Jesse had taken Maya home, Tina had left with Doyle. The two of them had become an item ever since, and as word had it, Tina had gotten pregnant with Doyle, their first son, only months after Maya had gotten pregnant with Benjamin. Maya had already been gone by then, but she'd seen the couple around town plenty of times. Although Tina and Doyle had two children together, they looked anything but happy.

"Benjamin, you can't go around—" The doorbell rang. Maya glanced at the door in disbelief. She hadn't even had time to speak to Benjamin about Jesse. "We'll talk about this later." Maya gave him a stern look, scribbled her signature onto his agenda, and handed it back to him.

"I don't see why you are so mad." Benjamin shoved his folder back into his backpack. "You always said not to let people bully me."

The doorbell rang again, followed by a firm knock. "I meant — tell the teacher or something." She took a deep breath and blew it out. "Stay right there. We have some things to discuss."

"Snitches get stitches," Benjamin mumbled as Maya headed for the door.

Maya whirled back around. "What did you say?" she asked as she whipped open the door.

"Snitches get stitches," Benjamin stood up boldly. "That's what Doyle said."

"Hey, buddy." Jesse stood on the other side of the door.

Benjamin grumbled and then stomped out of the room.

"What's wrong with him?" Jesse asked. "Looks like I'm not the only one having a bad day. And what's with the stitches thing? Isn't that a prison term or something?"

Despite the seriousness of her situation, Maya burst out into hysterical laughter.

Jesse stepped inside and placed a hand on her shoulder. "Are you okay?"

Maya sauntered back to the couch and flopped down. "I think I'm having a nervous breakdown."

"Okay." Jesse sat down beside her, so close that her already jumbled brain became even more jumbled. "One thing at a time. Let's start with Benjamin. What happened?"

18

———

JESSE

Maya gave Jesse the rundown on what had happened between Benjamin and Doyle III at school.

"A leech? Does Benjamin even understand what that means?"

"Does Doyle?"

"Well, of course not. He's just repeating what his parents said."

"You mean his mother? The girl you used to date. The girl you—"

"Okay, fine." Jesse relented. "But that was a long time ago. She can't still be upset about that." But she could, and Jesse knew it. Seeing Tina at the mall, he realized he had hurt her badly. And then there was Doyle, who had always insisted that Tina was not right for Jesse. He'd always known that Doyle had had a crush on her, but seeing them together was like watching oil and water trying to mix. But Jesse had bigger fish to fry — way bigger.

"It's true, Jesse. We don't belong in your world. Benjamin and I are just leeches. We've been living off your mother all this time and even before then, I never belonged in that school."

"That's stupid, Maya. You got into that school on scholarship because you're smart. You earned it and deserve an education as much as anyone else. And Benjamin—" Jesse looked up to see Benjamin standing in the doorway. Overwhelmed with love for the boy, he said, "My son deserves the best, and that's what he's going to get."

"You are my dad!" Benjamin cried. "I knew it!"

Maya sat back and watched the display. Her eyes told Jesse to tread lightly. It was clear her only care in the world was her son's well-being. Setting aside the adoration he had for her, he held a hand out to his son. "I am."

Benjamin took a careful step forward and around the couch, coming to a stop in front of Jesse. He was so brave and bold. Braver than his father, who had abandoned his one and only son. If only he'd have known.

"I've missed so much of your life. I hope you can forgive me."

Benjamin nodded, his eyes glistening with tears as he put on a tough face for his father. Seeing him like that, reminded Jesse of all the years he'd tried to please his own father but had failed repeatedly. Without another moment, Jesse pulled Benjamin into his chest and hugged him. "Never again, buddy. Never again. You're stuck with me now."

Maya put a hand on Benjamin's shoulder. "Baby, we need to keep this a secret for now. Do you understand?"

"From Doyle?" Benjamin sniffled as he looked up at his mom.

"Well, yes. From Doyle, too. But I was talking more about Mrs. James. Just until we figure out what to do."

Jesse knew it was burning Maya to look her son in the eyes and tell him to keep such a huge secret, but at the moment it was for the best. Jesse's life was more uncertain than it had ever been. He'd spent his adult life denying Weiland James was his father, and now — it was possible that he wasn't.

"Why can't Mrs. James know? She will like — oh!" Understanding lit his son's face. "Is she your mom?"

"She sure is, buddy. That means that she's your grandmother."

"But how come she never told me about you? How come you didn't?" Benjamin turned to his mother.

"We were trying to protect you, buddy." Maya ruffled his hair. "I'm sorry for not telling you the truth."

Benjamin took a step back. "Are you a bad guy?"

"No. Of course not." Jesse's heart hurt for the boy. "It's kind of complicated."

"Then why?" The boy placed his hands on his hips, making Jesse smile.

To Jesse's relief, Maya took over before he could try to explain. "Honey, I was very young when… well," Maya looked at Jesse for help.

"Your mom and I were in love, buddy." Maya's eyes widened, but Jesse didn't care. It was true. He'd loved Maya and there was nothing she could say to make him believe she hadn't felt the same way for him. At least back then. "But your mom and I, we made a —" How could he tell his son that he'd made a horrible decision that night, when the product of that decision was sitting right in front of him, and he was an amazing little boy.

"We made a handsome young man," Maya finished. "And we don't regret it one bit. But we weren't ready for you, Benjamin. We… I didn't tell him that you…" Maya looked up at Jesse. "I guess I've made a mess of things."

"It's okay, Mom. You're still the best mom, no matter what."

Jesse watched the little guy as he spoke to his mother with such love and affection. And he was smart too. Benjamin had gotten all of his qualities from Maya. And now that he knew the truth, that Weiland James was possibly not his father, Jesse was glad Benjamin had soaked in all the outstanding qualities from his mother's side of the family. As it was, Jesse's family roots were more unstable than a freshly planted tree.

"Let's get you a snack, buddy." Maya stood. "But don't think you are getting away with punching Doyle Anderson in the gut."

"You did that?" Jesse looked at his son with awe. "You socked him in the—"

"Jesse Carter James!" Maya admonished him. "My son is not a bully!"

"No fighting." Jesse lowered his eyebrows at his son, but couldn't keep the smile from his face. If Doyle the third was anything like his father, Benjamin would need to stand his ground. "Unless someone else starts it. Then you can—"

"Then you can tell the teacher!" Maya reprimanded them both.

"You heard the man." Jesse grinned. "Snitches get stitches!"

Maya shook her head, reprimanding him with her eyes. "You and I have some things to discuss."

Jesse placed his hands in the air. He'd only been officially a father for a few minutes, and already he was overstepping. "Your mom's right, buddy. Fighting is not the answer."

Jesse watched Maya as she got Benjamin fed, showered, and ready for bed. He stood at the door as she read their son a story and then tucked him into bed. His heart clenched when Maya prayed over their sleeping son, then got up quietly and left the room.

Jesse hadn't been much for religion until he joined the military. It was there that he'd learned of a higher power. He'd been so young when he'd joined. So scared and naïve of the world. And there he was - eighteen and ready to conquer it. He'd not been as tough as he thought he was, and when a fellow recruit had sat down beside him on the plane from bootcamp to their first duty station in Seattle, Jesse had learned that there was a man out there who was bigger than any other man, stronger than any bullying father, and loved more than any human being could ever love. On that short flight from San Diego to Seattle, Jesse James had found meaning in his life. And here - Maya Brown, a girl he'd admired and loved, was praying to the same God he'd only recently come to know. It was almost as if it had all been a part of a bigger plan.

Maya walked into the living room, and Jesse followed. She flopped down onto the couch and Jesse sat beside her.

Placing her head in her hands, Maya shuddered as she released a wave of tears. She was overwhelmed and Jesse didn't know what to do for her. Putting his arm around her, he drew her close. "I'm sorry, Maya. I'm so sorry."

Maya sobbed into his shoulder for a long time before lifting her head. "I'm not cut out for this, Jesse. I'm not strong."

"You don't need to be strong." Jesse held her close. "I'll be strong for both of us."

At his words, Maya's body shuddered even more as she hid her face in his shoulder. Jesse had no idea what to do. With each word, he seemed to make her more upset.

A second later, Maya looked up with a gleam of laughter in her eyes. He'd finally pushed the poor girl over the edge. "You okay?"

Maya burst out into another round of half-laugh half-crying as she wiped her eyes on her shirt and sniffled. "I think I'm delirious!"

"You?" Jesse pulled her closer, loving the way she felt in his arms. "I just found out my father might not be my father."

Maya sat up and eyed him for a moment before speaking. "You really don't have many of his features. You take much more after your mother."

"Yeah. Well, according to him, my mom was stepping out on him in the beginning of their marriage. My father says he's not even capable of having children." Jesse still couldn't grasp the idea that all of this time, his parents had lied to him. It made sense, though. He'd never understood why his father hated him so. And now he knew...

"What are we going to do?"

That certainly was the question of the hour. When he'd first found out about Benjamin, he'd planned to storm into that hospital room and demand answers. If it hadn't been for promising Maya he wouldn't, he'd have gone and confronted his father, possibly ruining everything. "I'm not really sure yet. I've got to find out what all of this means." And the only simple solution was the death of Weiland James. Knowing what he now knew, Jesse didn't blame the man for never connecting with him and he certainly didn't want the man going to his grave with so much hate in his heart. "I need to speak to him. Make things right."

"Make things right?" Maya focused her dark chocolate eyes on him. "None of this is your fault, Jesse."

"Oh, but it is." And it was time for Jesse to stand up and be a man. "I'm going to do whatever I can to fix this."

"What are you going to do?"

Jesse knew what he had to do. "I'm going to file for that unique circumstances honorable discharge, and I'm going to take over the business for my father." Even if Weiland was not his father, he was the only man Jesse had ever known, and Jesse had done everything he could from the time he was young, to get under the man's skin. Maybe it was that his father had always kept a safe distance, or maybe it was that his mother had protected him from every one of his father's outbursts, making Weiland the enemy. With his new perspective, Jesse saw his life in a totally different light. Nothing was as it seemed.

"What if he doesn't want you to? What if he…"

"We are going to need to keep Benjamin quiet for just a little while longer. I need time to make amends with him… or at least try." It was the right thing to do. Whether or not the man was his father, he had taken care of Jesse. Maybe he didn't love him like a real father would, but he had stepped up and took care of him, regardless. That was worth something.

19

————

MAYA

Maya stood at the window and watched Benjamin get into the limo with Constance. Mrs. James had called the night before and requested to spend the day with Benjamin, and of course, Maya was in no position to refuse.

Benjamin waved up at her and Maya blew him a kiss. "I love you, baby," she mouthed as he got into the car.

The door closed and Maya waved as the driver drove away. Maya pulled her phone out and called Hailey. Her nerves were frayed, and she didn't know if she was doing the right thing. Nothing seemed to be the right thing anymore.

"Hey, girlie. How'd it go with you-know-who?"

"You can say his name, Hailey." Maya let out a nervous chuckle. "Repeating it will not bring on a curse."

"You could have fooled me. That name is bad luck in this town. The other day I was in the grocery store, and he came in. No one said anything, but I swear people were worried he was going to rob the place or something."

Maya chuckled. "He was a wild kid. At one time, he and Doyle had the entire town looking over their shoulders."

"Why is everyone so afraid of those two? It's not like —"

"Like their fathers could sweep anything under the rug? It's exactly like that."

"Right. I guess I wouldn't know. So how's Benjamin taking the news?"

"Amazingly. It's crazy to see him interact with Jesse. They are so much alike that it's scary."

"You think he'll tell Mrs. James?"

Maya shook her head with a sigh. "I didn't have the heart to remind him of our secret. It just doesn't seem right to make him lie for me." It wasn't right, and Maya had lost a great deal of sleep just thinking about it. In the end, she'd decided not to mention it. "I'm just going to rely on God to straighten everything out."

"Sounds like you're taking a pretty big chance."

"What does that mean?" Maya retorted.

Hailey didn't believe in God. She'd made that clear from the first time Maya had got into her cab. God was a concept. An idea. One Hailey didn't believe in. "I'm just saying… I mean, say God is real. Do you really think He cares about what is happening in your life? Do you think He cares whether Benjamin knows who his father is or not? Or whether Jesse is the heir of a multi-billionaire?"

"Yeah. I think He does." Maya had spent a good deal of time praying over Benjamin. She had no doubt that God loved her.

"I think you should put more of your trust in making sure Benji keeps quiet. Mrs. James is the one who wields all the power in this situation."

"She has no more power than that which is given to her." Although the words came out in confidence, Maya wasn't sure of anything anymore.

"Doesn't God hate money or something like that?" Hailey asked.

Maya laughed. "He doesn't hate money, Hails. He just warns that the love of money can lead to destruction."

"Same thing," Hailey mumbled, then changed the subject. "So, what's the plan?"

Maya let the 'God' subject go for the moment. She had more battles to fight than trying to convince Hailey that there was a God and that He cared about her. Maya had planted plenty of seeds over the years. Only God could water them. "I'm not sure. Jesse seems to have a plan up his sleeve."

"So, what do you need me for?"

"Duh! Spying, what else?"

"Now you're talking." Hailey gave a maniacal laugh. "Get your shoes on. I'll be there in five."

Hailey hadn't even asked who they were spying on or why, but Maya knew she wouldn't. The girl loved to get in the middle of things. That was why she enjoyed being a taxi driver.

True to her word, Hailey pulled up out front five minutes later and honked her horn. Slipping on her shoes, Maya grabbed her purse and headed out the door.

"What's our first stop?" Hailey asked as Maya climbed into the passenger seat. "I've got an hour and—" She checked the clock. "Twenty-two minutes before I have to go back on the clock."

From Benjamin's usual description of his Saturday visits with Mrs. James, Maya made a decision. "Where do they serve smiley-face pancakes?"

"Uh, only half the restaurants in town. How can you think about food at a time like this, anyway?"

"Not for me, silly. Mrs. James usually takes Benjamin out to breakfast in the morning. Wherever she takes him, he always has the smiley-face pancakes."

"Oh." Hailey pulled out into the street. "Why didn't you say so?"

Ten minutes later, Hailey and Maya were pulling up into *Bac'n Eggs*, the local, all-day breakfast place. "There's the limo." Hailey pointed to an area in the back of the lot.

Maya ducked.

Hailey pulled the taxi around the lot and right up next to the limo.

"What are you doing?" Maya screeched, ducking lower.

"Get up, silly. They aren't in there."

Maya popped up her head and came face-to-face with Henry, the James family butler. Maya's eyes grew wide and so did his. "I thought you said no one was in there?" She popped her head back down, knowing full well that she looked guilty doing so.

Hailey rolled down the passenger window.

"What are you doing?" Maya screeched.

"Hi, Henry!" Hailey called, waving like some kind of lunatic.

"Remind me to read you the dictionary definition of spying," Maya grumbled.

"Henry, are Mrs. James and Benji inside?"

"Yes, Miss Hailey. They went in about ten minutes ago. They should be in there for a little while longer."

Now that her head was stuck into her lap and Hailey was having a conversation with Henry, Maya was too embarrassed to bring her head back up so she stayed where she was, hoping Henry hadn't gotten a good look at her.

"Thanks, Henry." Hailey waved. "How's Melly doing?"

"Seriously?" Maya grumbled.

"Melly is feeling better. I'm sure she'd like a visit from you."

"I'll get by either tonight or tomorrow morning."

"Okay then." Henry called back. "I'll tell Melly to look for ya."

"Thanks, Henry!"

"Behave yourself, girl." Henry said as Hailey placed the car in drive. "You too, Miss Brown!"

"Seriously?" Maya grumbled. "Bye, Mr. Henry." She waved a hand in the air but did not lift her head up until Hailey had pulled fully out of sight.

"How do you know Henry?" Maya asked, smoothing out her clothes.

"Henry is Melly's grandpa. Everyone knows he works for the James' family."

"Oh." Maya said as if that made perfect sense. "I hope he doesn't tell Mrs. James we were here."

"He won't." Hailey found a space on the side of the restaurant building out of sight of the general public. "I can just imagine that conversation, though." Hailey let out a laugh as she placed the car in park.

Mrs. James could be very demanding. She was a woman who

knew how to manipulate any situation to suit her. Maya didn't imagine Mrs. James would find interrogating her employees below her. Then again, she couldn't ask about what she didn't know.

"So, what do we do now?"

"Watch?" Hailey asked. "I mean, what are we spying on them for anyway?"

"I want to see if Benjamin tells her and possibly gauge her reaction."

Hailey glanced into the side window of the restaurant. "Hmmm. you don't think she'll freak out on him, do you?" Before Maya could answer, Hailey answered her own question. "Nah. Mrs. James is tough, but she loves Benji too much to hurt him."

"You think so?" Maya didn't believe Mrs. James was capable of hurting a child either, especially not her own grandson. Benjamin did not completely understand the concept of family. He understood that Jesse was his father and that Mrs. James was Jesse's mother, but he didn't exactly equate that to the fact that all of those factors meant Mrs. James was his grandma.

"Mrs. James can be crazy, but she'd never hurt Benjamin." Hailey turned to look at Maya. "At least not directly."

"That's what I'm afraid of." Maya searched the tables inside to find her son, but the place had several areas that were out of her view. Benjamin could be sitting at some secluded table way in the back, and if Maya knew Mrs. James as well as she thought she did, she wouldn't want to be seen by the average pedestrian walking by.

"Here they come." Hailey grabbed Maya by the neck and pulled her behind a row of bushes.

"Ouch!" Maya cried out as her knees hit the cold cement. "You're strong, Hailey! Do you work out or something?" Lifting her knees from the ground and going for a squat position, she rubbed at her knees.

"Shhhhh." Hailey motioned by putting a finger to her lips and ducking lower. "They're coming past."

Maya lowered her head and waited for them to pass. Her legs tingled as the blood seemed to be stuck below the knees in her current position. "I really need to join a gym," Maya whispered as

Henry drove up and idled the car in front. Mrs. James guided Benjamin to the back seat and Constance buckled him into the car.

"Constance, could you give me a moment? I need to make a call before heading out."

"Sure, Mrs. James. Benjamin and I will pick out a movie while we wait."

"Who is she calling?" Hailey whispered.

"I don't know." Maya dipped her face up to get a look. "What if she's calling–" Maya's phone blurted out with the song — *Cruella Deville.*

"Shut it off!" Hailey grabbed Maya's purse. "Shut it off!"

Mrs. James stopped and looked around as Maya struggled to find her phone in her purse. Mrs. James was almost on top of them as her phone burst out with the lyrics — *If she doesn't scare you ...*

Hailey slapped a hand over her mouth. "Hurry up!"

Maya finally got her phone in her hand and silenced it. Mrs. James pulled her phone away from her ear and looked at her phone, then put it back to her ear and spoke. "Maya, this is Mrs. James. Please call me back ASAP."

Maya turned to look at Hailey. "Do you think she knows?"

Hailey shook her head and slid a finger across her neck with wide eyes. If Hailey hadn't suggested she was dead, Maya would have already known. They watched as Mrs. James climbed into the limo next to Benjamin and Henry drove off.

Maya got to her feet, and Hailey pulled her back down. "Wait until the car is out of the lot at least."

Maya waited a little longer, her lower legs tingling all the way down to her toes. "Do you think she knows?"

Hailey peeked up over the bushes and then stood, shaking out her legs. "I don't know. She didn't look upset or anything. Maybe she just wants to talk?"

"Right." Maya stood up too fast and her legs buckled and stung. "Mrs. James never calls me just to talk." Bending down, she rubbed her legs, hoping to get rid of the tingling.

"Stomp your feet." Hailey demonstrated by stomping her own. "It'll get the blood flowing again."

Maya followed suit, feeling her limbs slowly coming back to her. "Should I call her back now?"

"You know her better than I do. Will she freak out if you don't?"

"I better call her." Maya and Hailey walked back to Hailey's taxi and Maya stared at the preset widget to dial Mrs. James. The only thing that continued to run through her mind was that Mrs. James knew. Benjamin had told her, and now she was going to throw them both out on the streets. Mrs. James never called when she spent the day with Benjamin unless he was hurt, and it was obvious that Benjamin was not hurt.

"Are you going to call or not?"

"I'm scared." Maya stared out the window. "Maybe I should wait her out?" If only she could call Jesse and ask him what he thought. He would know what to do, but Jesse was currently at the hospital with his father and things were probably not going so well for him either.

"Your death." Hailey started the car.

"Hailey!"

"I'm just saying." Hailey placed the taxi into reverse and backed out of her space. "Maybe it's nothing. But if you don't call her back, what kind of mom does that make you look like? What if Benjamin was hurt? Wouldn't you want to know?"

"He's not hurt, Hailey. I just saw him."

"I know that, and you know that, but Mrs. James doesn't. Well, that is, if you didn't blow it with that crazy ringtone." Hailey burst out laughing.

Hailey was right. If Maya didn't call Mrs. James back, Mrs. James would think she was inattentive to her own son's needs. "Okay. I guess you're right." Maya's fingers shook as she pressed the Icon with Mrs. James number attached to it.

"Oh, Maya!" Mrs. James' voice seemed out of breath. "Where have you been?"

"I'm sorry, Mrs. James. I wasn't able to answer the phone. Is Benjamin okay?"

"He's fine. I'm going to need to drop him off a little early today, so I just wanted to be sure you were home when we arrive."

"Oh." Maya took in a deep breath and mouthed to Hailey - It's okay. "I am just down the street. I can be back at my apartment in five minutes."

"Oh, you don't have to come back so quickly. I'm going to take him by the toy store and let him pick out a toy and then to the clothing store. He's growing so quickly. I'd like to grab him a couple new outfits."

"You don't have to do that, Mrs. James." Maya had never said those words before. She'd always just allowed Mrs. James to buy whatever she wanted for Benjamin, but now… things had taken on an enormous change, and Maya wasn't sure she wanted to be in for any more debt to the James family.

"Nonsense! We're at the store now. I'll drop him off shortly after lunch."

Maya agreed and hung up the phone. Turning to Hailey, she pushed out a dramatic sigh. "She doesn't know." Frustration warred with guilt inside of her.

What kind of mother was she to make her own son lie? Then again, hadn't Mrs. James forced her to lie to Benjamin all of this time? What made anything so different now?

20

JESSE

Jesse sat in the chair at the end of his father's bed and watched his chest rhythmically rise and fall. The thought that the man might not be his father had never in his wildest dreams occurred to him. Could it possibly be true? It sure would explain the tension in their home. From the time Jesse was a small child, his father had always kept him at arms-length.

When he'd questioned his mother, she refused to speak of it. "He is your father, Jesse. There's nothing left to tell."

His father's eyes fluttered open and Jesse checked to see if he was finally awake or only stirring. The conversation was one Jesse wanted to avoid at all costs, but knowing what he now knew, he owed it to his father to listen. He couldn't imagine what his father had gone through all these years thinking his son was not his, if that were the case.

His father's eyes focused on him for a moment, and then he turned his face to the window. "What are you doing here?"

"I just want to talk, Dad."

"Did your mother tell you?"

"Tell me what?" Jesse stood and went closer. "That you're not my father? She says you are."

"Of course she does." His father's face turned and his eyes penetrated Jesse's. "But I can't have children. Never could. I've known this since I was a teenager."

"What do you mean?" For the first time in many, many years, it surprised Jesse to hear his father speaking to him with a level of calmness. "How did you know?"

"It's a long story. Your mother knew nothing about it but the doctor assured me I could never have children."

"What happened, Dad?"

His father stared out the window, unspeaking. Just when Jesse was sure he would not tell him, his father spoke. "I was sixteen. Five black teens jumped me in an alley behind my father's building. They beat me up so badly that I couldn't walk for a week. One of them - he kicked me so hard in the groin that I thought I would die. The doctor told me it would be a miracle if I ever was able to father a child."

The image of his father being beaten down by five black teenagers was like a punch in the gut to Jesse. Everything seemed to fall into place. His father didn't just hate black people. He held a grudge for a race because a few teenagers had caught him in a back alley and beat the tar out of him. That, of course, seemed unreasonable, but his father was from a different time. He'd grown up in an era where racial tensions were still thick and a person didn't have to justify their hate. They didn't even have to disguise it as many did now.

"Have you ever gotten a DNA test done? Is it possible the doctor was wrong? Did he say it was an impossibility that you could ever have children?"

"My office." A tear dropped down his father's cheek. "I've never opened it. I wanted you to be my son, Jesse. I just don't think…"

"You never opened it?" His lips parted in surprise. Who does that? Who goes through the trouble of getting a DNA test and then doesn't look at the results?

"Dad, I'm sorry. I never meant to be such a…" Jesse wiped his own eyes as they misted. "I was such a horrible kid. I gave you and Mom a hard time for as long as I can remember."

"It never mattered to me. You will always be my son. That's why I never opened the results."

"Then why are you so angry with me?" Jesse pulled his chair closer and sat across from his father. "Dad, I don't care if you are biologically my father. You're the only man I've ever known." That his father had been so rough on him as a teenager meant nothing to him at the moment. He'd deserved at least most of the treatment his father had given him. He'd been a terror around the town, refused to listen to anyone in authority, and had embarrassed his father on more than one occasion. But Maya —

It would be easy for him to dismiss his father's treatment of Maya under any other circumstances than the one he was in. At the moment, Jesse had a little boy that he needed to be there for, and the only way to do that was to gain his father's approval.

"I have little time left on this earth. It seems I was wrong. Money cannot buy everything." His father lifted his head. "I need you to step up and take over the business."

"I will, Dad. I promise. Mom is looking into getting me some kind of special discharge. I don't know how long that will take, though. I might have to go back for a little while before—"

"Your mother thinks I don't know."

"Know what?"

"I have a grandson, don't I?"

Jesse watched his father for a moment, unsure whether it was some kind of trick. Could admitting his father's suspicion put him in an even more precarious position? Would his father disown him? And his mother — if she knew he knew, would she take it out on Maya?

"Benjamin. He's a handsome young man. I've seen the pictures on Ms. Brown's desk."

"You know?" Jesse stared at his father in awe. How had he known all these years?

"Of course I know. Your mother thinks she's running some kind of game on me, but she's not. I knew who she was from the moment I saw her."

"Then why the big secret?"

His father looked away again. "Your mother has invested so much time in the boy that I didn't want to ruin it for her. He's brought new life to her, given her a purpose. And..." His father coughed. "I knew someday it would bring you home. I just didn't know that I would be dying."

"I'm sorry, Dad. I've caused so much trouble, but Maya—"

"You love her, don't you?"

"I do. More than anything. Dad, I need your blessing on this. I want to marry Maya. I want to do right by her and Benjamin. It's the only thing I have ever wanted."

"Maya is a good girl." His father shifted in his bed. "She's been working for me for years now, and I have never had a better, more attentive secretary. And after what I put her through, she didn't have to be."

"That's just who she is. She's a great person, Dad. I know what you thought back then, but it's not true. Maya was not just another way to get under your skin. I cared about her back then, and I still do now."

His father nodded and swallowed. "Jesse. It doesn't really matter if you are my son or not. Soon I will be gone and everything I have worked for will belong to you. You are my son." A tear slid down his cheek. "I hope you can forgive me for the way I've treated you."

For the first time since Jesse was a young boy, he reached over and took his father's hand. "I love you, Dad."

"I love you too, son."

Jesse left the hospital more whole than he'd felt in a long time. He wanted to ask his father to talk to his mother about Maya and clear things up, but he couldn't put his father through that. He was dying after all.

Standing by his rental, Jesse leaned against the car and stared at the sky with a grateful heart. He had so much to be thankful for.

He'd been running for so long and so hard that he hadn't given himself time to think about the future. Now he had so much to consider. Maya, Benjamin, taking over the business for his father... smoothing things over with his mother. He just wasn't sure where to begin.

"Thank you, God."

His phone rang in his pocket, startling him. He pulled it out and saw Maya's smiling face looking back at him. Just the person he wanted to talk to.

"Hello, beautiful."

"How'd it go with your father?"

Jesse slipped inside his car and sat down. "He doesn't have long. We had a good talk, though. He knows about you and Benjamin."

"He what?" Maya's voice cracked. "Jesse! I told you no one can know! Mrs. James… your mother… what if she… oh, Jesse. This is not good."

"Calm down. It's okay. And I didn't tell him. He already knew."

"He already knew? What do you mean by that?"

"He's known all this time. All that time you've been working for him, he knew who you were."

"That's wild!" Maya cried. "He's really known all this time? Why has he never said anything?"

"He said something about it being my mom's project, and he didn't want to ruin it for her. I don't know. It makes no sense to me, but now I have another decision to make."

"What?"

"My father says there's a DNA test result somewhere in his office. He's never opened it, but had it done many years ago."

"Do you want to know?"

"I don't know." Did he want to know? Did it really matter now? So much of his life had been unduly stressed. "Maybe finding out the answer is not that important. I mean, what does it really matter? He's dying."

"Maybe you should wait then? I guess… I don't know." Her voice sounded stressed.

"What's going on? Are you still worried about my mother?"

"Of course I am. Jesse, you don't get it." Maya let out a breath. "You've spent all these years running while I've had to fend for Benjamin and myself all alone. I never wanted to take money from your mother. I never wanted any part of this at all. I just want to take care of…" Maya broke down in tears. "I'm sorry. I've got to go.

Benjamin will be home any minute, and I can't let him see me like this."

"Maya, wait."

"I can't, Jesse. He thinks I'm strong. He trusts me to take care of him. I'm not going to let him see me like this."

"I'm coming over right now."

"Jesse, no. Please. I just need some time to think and calm down."

"Later, then. After Benjamin has gone to bed. Can you get a sitter?"

21

———

MAYA

Maya disconnected the phone and went into the bathroom to wash her face before Benjamin got home. While Jesse was Benjamin's father, he didn't know how to take care of a child. Maya had spent many a night crying herself to sleep after a long, stressful day of pretending to be strong. She was tired of being strong. It took entirely too much energy.

She dried her face, put on some quick makeup, and then went to the window just in time to see the limo pull up with Benjamin. In a matter of days it seemed her world was falling apart, and it was all because Jesse had come home. Wherever he went, trouble seemed to follow.

Benjamin waved at her, and she waved back, then went to the door and waited for Constance to walk him up. As per usual, Constance was carrying a bag full of goodies for Benjamin. The boy was truly spoiled, but that was better than the alternative.

"Hi, Mom!" Benjamin dropped his coat onto the couch and ran from the room. "I gotta pee!"

"He's had to go for about three blocks now." Constance smiled as she handed the bag to Maya. "Just some new jeans. Mrs. James says he's growing out of his other ones."

"Thank you." Maya took the bag.

"I better get back down to Mrs. James." Constance turned to leave. "Have a good day, Maya."

Maya watched the woman leave, wondering what had changed to make her speak so politely to Maya.

Benjamin came out of the bathroom as Constance closed the door behind herself.

"Did you wash your hands?"

"Yep." Benjamin dried his hands on his shirt.

"Really? You took all that time to wash them, and now you're drying them on your dirty shirt?"

"It's not dirty." Benjamin placed his hands in the air for inspection. "See."

Maya sighed. She had no energy to make him go back into the bathroom and rewash his hands and dry them properly. "Why don't you go put your new clothes away, then."

It was over an hour later when Hailey finally returned Maya's text with a phone call. Maya was in the middle of cleaning the bathroom, her gloved hands armed with foaming bubble bathroom spray.

Pulling off a glove, Maya answered. "Hey, Hails. Give me one second." Maya put the phone on speaker so she could spray the toilet and the bathtub before pulling off her gloves. "Okay. I'll just let that sit for a minute while I talk to you. What's up?"

"You texted me. What's up?"

"Oh, right." Maya explained to Hailey that Jesse wanted to meet her after Benjamin went to bed to snoop around in Mr. James' office for some evidence of DNA.

"DNA? For who?"

"Shhh. Hailey, I'm probably not supposed to be spreading that around. Don't go repeating that." Maya looked around as if there could be someone listening.

"DNA for who?" Hailey whispered into the phone. "Benjamin?"

Maya giggled. After their morning spy session on Mrs. James, Maya and Hailey had agreed that counterintelligence was not their gig.

"For Jesse."

"Jesse?"

"I'm not sure of the details, but Jesse wants to find it and he doesn't want his mother to know. So, since I have a key to the office, he asked me to go."

"Yeah. I guess I can come by around nine. Are you sure this is a good idea though?"

Maya wasn't sure about anything at that point. "He asked me to go. Am I supposed to just say no?"

Hailey chuckled. "You got it bad, girl."

"No, I—"

"I don't blame you. Jesse is hot. And a military man!"

Maya pictured Hailey fanning herself and rolled her eyes. Maybe she did have it bad for him. Although she'd thought she'd gotten over him, she hadn't. From the moment he'd come back to town, her world had been spinning out of control. Just like the first time. Maya never seemed to learn.

"See you at nine?"

"Sure. I'll be there. I still think this is a bad idea, though. Mrs. James is going to flip when she finds out the two of you are sneaking around."

"Right?" It was dangerous, but when it came to Jesse — she'd never been able to resist him. Apparently, that hadn't changed. The only difference between then and now was that she had responsibilities. Now that she had Benjamin, nothing could take her focus from her child. Not even his father.

BENJAMIN WAS asleep by eight thirty. Maya kissed him on the forehead and snuck out the door. Hailey would be there soon, and Maya had forgotten to remind her to steer clear of the doorbell.

After changing her outfit several times, putting her hair up and then back down again, and applying some lip gloss to her lips, Maya looked in the mirror with a groan.

"What am I doing?" she asked, even though she knew the answer.

Maya was making a grave mistake. Mrs. James was Maya's only ally. She'd picked Maya up from the ground and taken her in after her mother died. Maya rubbed a hand along her neck. What she was about to do was risky and selfish. One false move and everything could blow up in their faces. Then Maya and Benjamin would be living on the streets.

No, Jesse wouldn't allow that. At least that's what she told herself. Jesse seemed sincere, but he hadn't been there for her when she needed him. How did she know he would be there for her now? That old image of Mr. James standing over them calling her out of her name while Jesse stared at his father, fear permeating from his pores. He hadn't stood up for her then.

Hailey was at the door at nine o'clock on the dot. Soon after Maya got her settled in, Jesse came to the door and the two of them were off to his father's office.

"Are you nervous?" Maya asked as she pulled on her seatbelt.

"Well, yeah. Kind of. I mean, what if he's not my dad?"

"You think that's possible?"

"My mom says there's no way he's not my father. My dad says he can't have kids."

"What if he's not?" Maya asked. "Will that change anything?"

Jesse glanced at Maya for a moment, and then his eyes went back to the road. "I don't know."

Finding out the truth could mean everything, or it could mean nothing. It seemed to Maya that it all depended on what Mrs. James wanted to do with the information. "If Weiland is your father, then that should solve all of our problems, right?"

"I guess so. I'm just not sure how my mom will react. She's used to controlling situations and if she can't, I just don't know what she will do."

Maya knew that was right. Mrs. James always had her hands in the family business. She wouldn't say so out loud, but Maya wouldn't put it past her to pull some crazy scheme on Mr. James to make him think he had a son. She looked at Jesse, trying to visualize his father in him. There was no trace of the man.

"Nothing, huh." Jesse turned to her. "I spent an hour looking in the mirror myself. We are as different as night and day."

"You both have brown eyes," Maya tried.

"Along with eighty percent of the rest of the world."

"Right."

Soon Jesse was pulling into the office building of W.C. James Manufacturing Co. It had only been a week since she'd spent her days filing papers for Mr. James, making his coffee, and running his errands. "He really knew all this time?"

"Knew what?" Jesse pulled into a space at the front of the building, designated for "CEO."

"I just can't believe he knew about me all this time and didn't even let on that he knew who I was."

"Kind of crazy, isn't it?"

"It just makes me so angry that —" Before Maya could finish, Jesse leaned in. Within a millisecond, Maya knew what he was about to do, but she was helpless to stop him. As soon as his lips met hers, she moaned. It was just like she remembered. So warm and soft. His hands touched her face, and she thought she would melt. Another moan escaped as Jesse deepened the kiss. How would she ever take control of her life if Jesse had her heart so wrapped around his finger that she couldn't even refuse a kiss from him?

Maya pulled away. "Not now, Jesse." *Be strong. Hold your ground.* "We need to figure out how to clean up this mess we are in first."

Jesse caressed her cheek for a moment before removing his hand. "I just want to be with you. Nothing else matters but you and Benjamin."

"I know, Jesse. I want us to be together too, but that might not be the right thing for... for Benjamin."

Jesse looked as if she'd slapped him in the face. "I am what's right for Benjamin. He's my son, and I have a right to be in his life."

Maya touched his leg. "I know. I get it. But we have to do this right. At the moment, you don't even know if you are Weiland's son. What if you aren't and your mother cuts you out of everything?"

Jesse seemed to search her face for the answers, but there was nothing there but fear. He placed his hand on hers that was still resting on his knee. "She won't cut me out. I'm still her son. At least I think I am."

22

JESSE

He'd said the words as if they were true, but in his heart, Jesse wasn't sure he believed them. Everyone thought of Claire James as the heart of the company. She was the one who organized charity functions, made donations, and organized benefits. It was her job, and she enjoyed it. But his mother was only satisfied when she was in complete control of a situation. Just as she was now.

"You ready to go inside?" Jesse asked, the warmth of her lips still lingering on his. "You brought the key, right?"

Maya nodded. "Ready if you are."

Jesse stepped from the car to open Maya's door, but she was out before he could get there. "How do you have a key to my father's office, anyway?" Weiland James didn't trust just anyone.

"Part of my job was to pick up fresh fruit and bagels each morning and bring them in for the upper echelon employees. Mr. James likes to have his coffee fresh and hot when he gets here. That's also part of my job."

"When I take over for him, will you make my coffee and bring me bagels?"

Maya pulled a set of keys from her pocket and slid one inside the lock. "Don't bet on it, Mr. James." Opening the door, she slid inside and pressed in a code to disarm the alarm.

Jesse followed her inside. A sense of nostalgia washed over him as he looked around. How many years had it been since he'd stepped foot inside his father's building? Ten? Eleven? It had been too long.

Maya headed toward the elevator, pressing on light switches as she went.

"Is that a good idea?"

Maya turned around. "Oh." She flipped off the lights. "It's just a habit."

"Thanks. I'd just rather not cause any undue attention." Even though he would take over for his father and had every right to be there, what they were doing seemed awry.

Once they exited the elevator and Maya opened the door to his father's office, his heart throbbed as if it could leap from his chest. He studied the office, eyes wide. Somewhere inside was an envelope that just might change his life.

"Where do we start?" Maya asked.

"He said it was in a filing cabinet." There was only one in the room, and it had a small silver lock on it. "You think that's it?"

"There are more down the hall, but this one is your father's private cabinet. If the evidence is here, I'm sure it would be inside this one."

"Okay, then. Let's see what we got." Jesse rushed toward the cabinet and squeezed the lever, but was unable to open it. "It's locked. Now what?"

Maya double-checked, yet the drawer refused to open. She shrugged. "I guess you're right. I think he keeps his keys in his top drawer." She stood, leaving her sweet scent to linger in the air. In a matter of seconds, her eyes lit up after discovering the key. Maya offered it to Jesse.

"You do it." Jesse nodded toward the cabinet.

"No way." Maya put her hands up. "I want nothing to do with breaking into Mr. James' personal files. In fact—" She tucked her hand in the end of her sleeve, wiping the keys on her jeans. Once the keys were wrapped in her sleeve, she pushed them toward Jesse. "Here. Take them. My prints are gone."

Jesse threw his head back and laughed. Once his amusement subsided, he dropped his gaze to admire Maya's stern face. Stubborn as always, she thrust the keys toward him. Jesse's lips twitched as she hid a grin. Without losing eye contact, he took the keys from her and set them on the filing cabinet. Before Maya could object, he took her in his arms and pulled her close. "I'm scared. Hold me."

"Stop that!" Maya giggled. "You're not scared one bit."

Jesse did his best to muster a serious look. "Hold me anyway?"

"Come on. Let's get this over with before someone calls the police on us."

Jesse retrieved the key from the cabinet and slipped it inside. "Wait. What do you mean? You silenced the alarm, right?"

"Yeah, but after that fire, your father put twenty-four-hour surveillance on this building."

Jesse swiveled around to face her. "Someone is watching us?"

Maya nodded. "Uh, most likely. But you are a James. No one would question you being in your father's office."

"Okay. True." Jesse unlocked and opened the drawer to shuffle through the files. Finding nothing in the top drawer, he moved to the next one. After another ten minutes of file-surfing, Jesse found a letter-sized, white envelope addressed to Weiland James. Jesse's heart hammered when he noticed the return address. *DNA Solutions.*

He pulled it out and set it on top of his father's desk. Before he was about to close the drawer, something caught his eye. A folder with two words written on top — Regina Brown — was sitting at the back of the drawer.

"Come get a look at this." Jesse called to Maya, who was sitting comfortably in his father's chair.

"What is it?" Maya stood and looked in the direction he was pointing. Her jaw dropped, and she glanced between Jesse and the file. Her mouth went dry. "Why does Mr. James have a file on my mother?"

"I don't know." Jesse pulled the file out and handed it to Maya. "Put it in your purse."

Maya shook her head and put her hands in the air. "No way, man. I'm not taking anything from this office."

"Not even if it has your name on it?"

"That's not my name."

"It's your mother's. Take it, Maya."

Maya shook her head again.

Just then steps sounded down the hallway. Maya looked over her shoulder in a panic.

"Take it!" Jesse shoved it at Maya.

Maya groaned. "Fine!" She ripped the folder from Jesse and shoved it in her purse. "Who do you think is coming?"

"I don't know." Jesse snatched the DNA envelope from the desk and sat in his father's chair, casually leaning back. Whoever was coming would be much less suspicious if he looked the part of a CEO. Following suit, Maya sat across from him.

Jesse used a letter opener from his father's drawer and opened the envelope. He'd come to see the results, and if whoever was coming down the hallway planned to stop him, he'd just as well see them before they got there.

Jesse pulled the letter from the envelope as the sounds of footsteps drew near. The second Jesse read the results, he noticed his mother's shadow.

"What are you doing in here?" she asked Jesse before averting her eyes at Maya. "You—" she pointed a finger at Maya, "I will deal with later."

Watching his mother treat Maya with such disregard had him jumping to his feet in shame. He wouldn't make the same mistake and let one of his parents belittle the woman he loved. This time, Maya would not have to fend for herself.

"You and Maya will have no dealings from now on, or I will walk out that door right now and never return." His face flushed with anger.

"You can't... we had a contract... she broke—" His mother refused to look at him.

"And when did you plan on telling me I have a son? What kind of contract keeps a father away from his boy?"

"That was for your own good. I was just trying to keep the peace. Your father would have turned them away if he found out about it. And who knows what he'd have done to you? He could have stricken you from his will. I did all of this for you, Jesse."

"For me? For me?" Jesse clenched his fists, taking a deep breath. "He's not even my father."

"What do you mean? Of course he's your father."

"Really?" Jesse gripped the letter, almost crushing it. He held it up to his mother. "Why does this say he's not?"

"What is that?" his mother snatched the paper to examine it. "Where did you get this?"

"It's DNA results. Weiland had them done when I was a baby. He's always known he wasn't my father, hasn't he?"

His mother steadied herself on the corner of the desk, her face turning white. When she looked like she was about to faint, Jesse took her arm. "Sit down, Mom. Maya, can you get her some water?"

Maya stood with a nod. After a few minutes, she returned with a cold bottle of water. Ms. James took it from her without so much as a thank you. It was then that Jesse knew that although his mother had said it was over, it was far from it.

His mother took a couple sips of water before speaking. "We'd been married for over two years. No matter what I tried, I couldn't get pregnant. Your father never told me he couldn't have children, or I never would have done it." She turned a pair of loving eyes on her son. "But I don't regret it. I will never regret having you."

"What did you do?" Jesse sat down, almost defeated. "Did you have an affair on Dad?"

"What?" His mother fanned her face. "No, of course not. I went to a fertility clinic. Of course, they didn't want to do it at first. Not without your father's approval, but money talks. After a significant donation to their clinic, they agreed to do the procedure."

"So you don't know who my father is?" Jesse stared at his mother in awe. Who did stuff like that? At least, if his mother was telling the truth, she hadn't cheated on his father.

"No, of course not. I got to choose some basic features, but I don't know the man."

Jesse looked at Maya, who stared at the two of them with her mouth wide open. He turned back to his mother. "And my dad has no idea that you did this."

"No. Of course not. He thinks you're his son."

Jesse forced back a chuckle. "I hate to break this to you, but obviously he doesn't." Jesse held up the envelope with his father's name printed in bold, black ink.

"This was addressed to your father? How did he——"

"It was unopened." Jesse set the envelope down. "He never opened it, but he suspected."

"You can't tell him." Her eyes pleaded with him. "He only suspects. He doesn't know for sure. Please. You can't tell him."

"You knew he suspected?"

"Well, yes. After I got pregnant was when he decided to tell me that horrible story about being jumped by a group of African Americans and not being able to produce, but I assured him that the doctor was wrong. He believed…" She looked down at the envelope. "I guess he didn't."

"He knows everything, Mom. How you shoved Maya down his throat by hiring her as his secretary. He knows he has a grandson and that you've taken care of everything for them." His eyes blurred. "And he knows he's not my father."

His mother bowed her head. "I see I've made quite a mess of things."

23

———

MAYA

Maya sat on her couch in her apartment and stared at the file in her lap. What was Mr. James doing with a file on her mother?

"Are you going to open it or try to read it by absorption?"

"Very funny." Maya tried to smile, but the pit in her stomach told her if she opened the file, she might open a can of worms. "You open it."

"No way. I already opened one envelope containing bad news."

"Speaking of... Do you think your mother is really going to just forgive me of my debt?"

Jesse thought about it for a second. "When she makes me CEO, I'll just pay it for you. How about that?"

"Why do I get the feeling it's not that easy? I mean, she doesn't have to make you CEO, does she?"

Jesse eyed her as if she had another head sprouting from her neck. "Why wouldn't she? Maybe I'm not Weiland's son, but I am hers."

"I don't know. I just have this nervous feeling in the pit of my stomach."

"That's what's making you nervous. Open it up and get it over with. It's probably nothing."

"Rip it off like a bandaid?"

"On the count of three," Jesse teased, then began to count. When he reached three, Maya opened the folder but squeezed her eyes shut.

"It's a police report." Jesse picked up the top page. "Why did my father have this?"

Maya opened her eyes and took the page from him. She skimmed the page, remembering the break-in that took her mother's life. She read the details - Home invasion/murder - victim identified as thirty-eight-year-old Regina Brown. Cause of death - blunt force trauma. Her mother had been killed, but nothing in the house had been taken. They had labeled it a burglary, but nothing about it made any sense. That Mr. James had a copy of the report made even less sense.

"That's a good question." Maya yawned. It was after midnight. "Maybe everything will make more sense in the morning?"

"Yeah. I guess I better get home before my mother sends the national guard out looking for me. I'm sure she wants to assure me again that all of her lies and manipulation was part of a bigger plan to save the world from domination."

"What's domination?" Benjamin stood in the doorway.

"Hey, buddy." Maya smiled. "What are you doing up?"

"I just wanted to say hi to my dad."

Maya tried to hide the shock at her son's words. Before she could answer him, Jesse stood. "Why don't I put you back in bed and we can talk for a while?"

"Do you like The Avengers?" Benjamin asked, making Maya's heart swell.

"Of course I do." Jesse put a hand on his son's shoulder. "Who's your favorite?"

"Either Hulk or Tony Stark. Black Panther is pretty cool too, though."

"Yeah? I like those too. You know who my favorite is, though?" Jesse winked at Maya.

"Who?"

"Captain America."

"Oh! I love him too!"

While the two of them walked down the hall, Maya turned back to the file. Underneath the police report were a couple other papers of no real importance. Until she got to the last double-folded page. Maya looked up to her son's bedroom where he and Jesse were speaking in whispers. She studied the paper with unease. Something about it didn't sit right, yet she didn't know why unless she opened it.

Once open, she stared at it in shock. When she finally found her voice, she called, "Jesse!"

Jesse came running down the hallway. "What's wrong?" Benjamin was right behind him.

"Let's get you to bed, buddy." Maya handed Jesse the paper and steered her son back to his bedroom. Just before they reached the room, Maya looked back. Jesse was staring at the page in stunned silence.

"Why can't my dad put me to bed?" Benjamin asked as he flopped onto his bed.

"Another time, I promise. Your dad and I need to talk about some things right now." She pulled his legs around and the blankets over him. Kissing him on the forehead, she said, "It's time for you to be a big boy and go to sleep."

"Big boys get to stay up." Benjamin grumbled, but turned on his side and closed his eyes.

"I love you, Benjamin." Maya kissed his cheek, pulled his covers up around his neck, and left.

When she returned to the living room, she found Jesse in the same position she'd left him in. Leaning against the wall, staring at the paper she had handed him.

"Why would my father's company pay for your mother's funeral and burial?"

"I don't know." Maya had only been sixteen. She'd had no idea where the money came from and had been too upset to ask. All she'd known was that they had given her mother a quiet funeral, and a shaded plot in the local cemetery. "Nothing makes sense anymore."

"I don't like this." Jesse took her hand. "Not any more than you do, but I think maybe we should keep this quiet for a while."

Maya agreed. Although the entire folder stunk of suspicion, there wasn't any evidence of foul play. Still, she couldn't help but wonder why the James' decided to help with something so monumental, like her mother's funeral, when she wasn't good enough for their son. "Jesse, how do you think your mom found out about my pregnancy?"

"What do you mean? You didn't go to her?"

"No, of course not. Do you ever listen to me?"

"I listen to you." He waited only a second before saying, "What did you say?"

Maya rolled her eyes. "I said she just showed up one day at the group home the state threw me in. She got me out of there and shipped me off to a school for pregnant girls. I was so grateful for what she did that I never asked her how she knew."

Jesse rubbed his chin. "Hm. Strange."

"That's all you can say?"

"Well, what are you thinking? How do you think she found out?"

"What if—" Maya refused to give the words validation by voicing them. "No. I don't know. I don't want to believe—"

"Believe what?"

"I don't know. There's no reason Ms. James would step in to help me unless she felt bad for something."

"Feel bad for what?" Jesse scratched his head. "Maybe for how my dad treated you?"

Maya gave him an incredulous look. "Really? Do you think she'd save me from a life on the streets just because your dad was mean to me?"

"Well, he was really wrong to treat you that way." He caressed her face.

"But still… that wouldn't be enough to make her do something as drastic as providing a life for me and Benjamin." Maya's heart clenched as a sense of awareness overcame her. "No…" Maya's face drained of color.

When Jesse saw how pale she'd become, he grabbed her hand.

"Are you okay? What is it?" He searched her dull eyes.

"She gave us a life. What do you do for someone when one life has been taken?"

Jesse let out a breath and ran a hand over his face. "No." He squeezed his eyes shut. "Surely not."

"What if…" Maya couldn't finish the sentence.

"You think my mom killed yours, don't you?" Jesse's voice broke, and Maya wondered if he thought the same thing.

"Well, why else would they have this paperwork? Your mom is keeping all these secrets from your dad, but your dad knows about them, anyway." She swallowed and wiped away her tears. "Your dad had been keeping it a secret that he knows about your mom's secrets. Why? There has to be a reason."

"And that reason is that my mother is a murderer?" A vein pulsed on his forehead.

"Maybe not your mother." Maya raised an eyebrow. "Maybe your father found out that I was pregnant and tried to have me exterminated, only he got my mother instead."

"Oh, stop it with the conspiracy theory stuff." Jesse took a breath. "I know my parents. They may be misguided, but neither of them could be capable of murder. The police report confirms a case of breaking and entering. I just don't get why my father has a copy of it."

"The question of the hour." Maya sighed, missing her mother more than anything. She had no idea what she would do if she ever found out who had taken her life early. Her mother would have loved Benjamin and he would have adored her. If Mrs. James hadn't stepped in, they would have had a far different life than what they have now. No, if anything, she was grateful to her. Maya chastised herself for ever thinking Mrs. James a murderer.

24

JESSE

esse's hand shook as he pressed Maya's phone number and waited for it to ring. Maya was going to be floored to hear what he was about to ask her. He still hadn't gotten over the shock of it himself.

"Hello?" Her sweet voice came on the line, making Jesse's heart skip a beat. He'd never tired of hearing her voice.

"Hey."

"Hey, Jess. What's up?"

"Where's Benjamin?"

"He's right here." Her voice sounded guarded. "What's up?"

"I have someone who wants to meet him."

"What? Who?"

"His grandfather."

Silence.

"Maya?"

"Oh, I don't know about that. I don't think I'm ready—"

Jesse shifted as he looked around the hospital parking lot. "He doesn't have much time left. He wants to meet his grandson."

"Did you tell him you opened the envelope?"

Jesse switched the phone to his left hand and wiped his right one on his jeans. "No. I'm not going to."

"What if he asks?"

"Don't push this, Maya. It's too much."

"Okay. I'm sorry. You're right."

"Can I come pick you and Benjamin up? We can go out to dinner after."

"I guess so. What do I tell Benjamin?"

"Tell him the truth. He's going to meet his grandfather."

Maya sighed. "Okay. Give me time to talk to him. We'll be ready in half an hour."

Jesse thanked her and hung up. Just as he pressed the end button, his phone rang. It was his mother again. She'd called him at least fifteen times since she'd caught them in his father's office, and Jesse had refused to answer all of them. He'd taken a chance by going up to the hospital to see his father, knowing that his mother would probably leave long enough to get some food into her system. Jesse had timed it almost perfectly. He'd only had to duck once as she passed him in the lobby.

Jesse hit ignore on the call, got into his rental, and headed to the gas station before going to Maya's apartment. Nervous was not even close to what he felt when he thought about bringing Benjamin to see his grandfather.

Technically, Weiland James was nothing to either of them, but he was the only father Jesse had ever known, and as harsh as he was, Jesse loved him. The man had raised him as his own and he was dying. What harm was it to Jesse to be kind to the man who'd passed an entire dynasty down to him.

It was such a release to discard all the hate and anger that had built up inside of him. He no longer held onto any of it and it felt good to not allow hate to rule his emotions.

When Jesse pulled in front of Maya's apartment, Benjamin popped in the window and waved. Jesse waved back, his heart swelling at the sight of his son. So many years had been lost. He'd missed his son's first words, his first steps, his first day of school. Everything, he'd missed everything.

There's still time, Jesse reminded himself. There were still many more firsts to come, and Jesse planned to be there for all of them.

Soon Maya stepped out with Benjamin at her side. She looked gorgeous, and Benjamin was as handsome as ever. Jesse didn't deserve either of them. He'd messed up so much in his life that he couldn't believe he was getting a second chance with the one and only girl who made his heart feel like it was under attack.

Maya loaded Benjamin's booster seat into the backseat, and Benjamin climbed in and buckled himself in.

"You ready to meet your grandfather?" Jesse asked.

"I think so." Benjamin looked at Jesse in the rearview mirror. "I hope he's not too mean."

Jesse raised an eyebrow at Maya, and she covered her mouth with a giggle. "Sorry. I might have called him a bear once or twice."

"She said Mr. James growls!" Benjamin called up front. "Like a big grizzly bear!"

Maya stretched to see her son in the backseat. "You stop telling those stories. Haven't I always told you that Mr. James was a good person for giving your mother a job?"

"Yeah. But not when he makes you work on Saturdays."

Maya laughed and turned back around like a child caught red-handed with a candy bar.

"You got a little chocolate on your face." Jesse chuckled. It was what she used to say to him when they were in high school and he'd tried to deny some prank he'd taken part in. She always knew when he was lying.

"Okay, okay. Fine. I might have been a little hard on your father, but after what we went through—"

"What bad things did she tell you about me?" Jesse teased, raising his eyebrows to his son in the backseat as he drove to the hospital. For a moment, a thought ran through his mind - What if she did bad-talk him? How awkward would that be for Benjamin being put on the spot?

"She said you are handsome, just like me."

Maya shrunk in her seat, inspecting her fingernails, ignoring the turn in conversation.

"She did, huh?" Jesse placed a hand on Maya's leg and squeezed.

"Yeah," Benjamin continued. "But I don't think I look like you at all. You're white!"

Maya burst into hysterical laughter and Jesse couldn't help the grin that formed on his face.

"Benjamin!" Maya called when she finally stopped laughing. "Where did you learn about that?"

"About what, Mom?"

"Skin colors!"

"People say it all the time. Doyle said I can't be white because my mom is black. He said even if my dad is—"

"Okay, young man. That's enough."

"What?"

Jesse squeezed Maya's leg again. It sounded like Doyle III was just like his father. "Hey, buddy." Jesse looked at his son through the mirror.

Benjamin made eye contact. "Yeah?"

"People should not be defined by their color, do you understand what I'm telling you?"

Benjamin started to nod, but then it turned into a shake of his head.

Maya gave Jesse a look as if to say that it was okay, but Jesse persisted.

"What I'm saying buddy is this…" He contemplated his words carefully. "God made all of us. Every single person in the entire world. He made our insides all the same. Our hearts, our minds. Our wants and desires." He patted Maya's leg and smiled. "Our dreams. Our feelings. Maybe you're too young to understand this now, but someday you will remember what I told you and you will understand. For now, son, never judge a person based on the color of their skin. Okay?"

"Okay."

It was amazing just how easy it was for Benjamin to agree. Maya had done an outstanding job with the boy. And no matter her motives, his mother was a key piece in Benjamin's life. Keeping the boy from his father was not a wonderful choice, but Jesse believed her heart, no matter how twisted, had been in the right place.

He pulled into the hospital parking lot and found a space. His nerves were like pinpricks as he, Maya, and Benjamin went into the hospital and took the elevator to the room where his father was slowly dying. Jesse said a quick prayer for his father to be in good spirits. He'd asked to see his grandson, but in his condition no one could begrudge him if he had an attitude. For Benjamin's sake, Jesse hoped the memory the boy had of his grandfather wasn't a grumpy, dying old man.

When they entered the room, it surprised Jesse to see his father's face fully shaved, his hair combed back, and the bed positioned so that he was at an almost sitting incline.

"Well, look who's got company." The nurse smiled as she checked his father's vitals. "I knew we were getting ready for company, but who knew we'd have such a handsome young man joining us."

"That's my grandson, Gloria."

"Your grandson? Weiland, where have you been hiding him all this time?"

Weiland smiled at the woman. "Give us a minute, would you?"

"Sure." Gloria smiled at each of them, then bent down to Benjamin and pinched his cheeks. "I thought I might need this." She handed Benjamin a lollipop.

"Thank you." Benjamin politely took the sweet treat and Gloria retreated from the room.

"Hey, Dad. How are you feeling?" Jesse stepped closer, pulling Maya and Benjamin to him. He would never again leave Maya feeling so alone and degraded in front of his father. Not in front of anyone.

"I'm okay, all things considered. It's this little guy here that I'm interested in getting to know." He smiled at his grandson. "How old are you, Benjamin?"

"I'm five." Benjamin spoke proudly. "How old are you?"

"Benjamin!" Maya gasped.

Weiland chuckled. "I'm fifty-four."

"Are you dying?"

Maya started to protest, but Weiland spoke before she could reprimand her son for his disrespectful curiosity.

"I am, son. And I'm afraid I haven't been a very good man. I hurt your mommy and daddy a bit. I just don't know how to make it up to them."

"Oh." Benjamin lowered his head for a moment. "Well, if you are going to heaven to be with Jesus, then everything will be all better. But you can't be with Him if you don't believe. You believe, don't you, Mr. James?"

A tear slid down Weiland's face, and then another. "I don't know much about Him."

"I can show you. My Sunday school teacher said it's never too late to ask. All you have to do is pray and tell Jesus that you believe in Him. Then you ask Him to forgive you of your sins and He will take it all away." Benjamin held out his arms. "As far as the east is from the west."

"Would you pray with me?" Weiland took his grandson's hand in his.

Jesse was so overwrought with emotion that he had to turn away as tears slid down his own face. Maya sniffled as she watched her son lead grumpy old Mr. James in the sinner's prayer. Leaning her head on Jesse, she buried her face in his chest and cried as Benjamin bowed his head and said the simplest prayer for his grandfather. Dutifully, Weiland repeated the words, asking Jesus to come into his heart.

It had been years since Jesse had said a similar prayer, asking God to guide him through his hurt and anger. He didn't know if his father meant what he was repeating or not, but Jesse hoped he did and one day he would see his father again in heaven.

25

______

MAYA

"He's not so mean at all!" Benjamin called from the backseat of Hailey's taxi.

Jesse had wanted to take them home, but Maya thought it was best he stayed with his father for the time being. She wanted to talk to Benjamin about what he'd done at the hospital, and Jesse needed to spend his father's last hours with him.

"He's not?" Hailey asked. "You mean he's not a big, ugly grizzly bear like I thought?"

"Nope. He was kinda nice. But why does Jesus want to take him to heaven so soon? I just got to meet him."

Maya turned around to meet her son's eyes. "I don't know why, buddy. Maybe Jesus has some important work for him to do." Maya worried Weiland had only repeated Benjamin's words for the sake of pleasing him, but she hoped it wasn't true. Even Weiland deserved a chance at redemption.

"Maybe he will want him to be a super spy or something." Benjamin sat up straight. "God has those, you know."

"How do you know?" Hailey asked, encouraging his imagination.

"Doyle said so. He said God has angels watching us to tell him if we've been bad."

Maya rolled her eyes. She was getting tired of Doyle. "God doesn't need spies to tell him if we are good or not. He already knows."

"He's like Santa Claus," Hailey teased.

"Nope." Benjamin popped up before Maya could respond. "Jesus is real and Santa Claus isn't."

"Let me guess. Doyle told you that too?" Hailey asked.

"No. Doyle doesn't know everything you know," Benjamin said. "He still believes in Santa." Benjamin covered his mouth and chuckled.

"Then how do you know?"

"Hailey!" Maya lowered her eyes. She didn't like the idea of Hailey interrogating her son about God.

"What?"

"*He* told me!" Benjamin pointed to the roof of the taxi with a huff. "Jesus told me that Mr. James needed to know how to get to heaven, and I told Him I would pray with him."

Hailey turned her head so quickly that Maya thought she might steer the car into a crash. "He talks to God?"

This was the first Maya knew about it. Sure, she brought her son to church, prayed with him each night and before meals, and read him stories from his big children's bible, but had he really spoken to God?

"All the time." She shrugged. Of course he talked to God. She just had no idea that God was answering him in such an audible way.

"Hm." Hailey shrugged her shoulders. "Maybe there's something to this God thing."

"Maybe you're right." Maya grinned. Benjamin was a regular evangelist. Before the day was out, he'd have guided two lost souls down the path to salvation — the heart of a child.

Just as Hailey pulled up to the apartment, Maya's phone rang. When she pulled it from her purse and saw Jesse's name, her breath caught.

"Hey, what's going on?" she asked as she got out of the taxi and handed Hailey payment for her ride. Usually Mrs. James paid for her rides, but she wasn't about to ask for anything at the moment. She still wasn't sure where she stood with the woman.

"He's gone." Jesse sniffled.

"Oh, Jesse." Maya took her son's hand and waved at Hailey as she drove off. "I'm so sorry."

Shudders sounded through the line as Jesse released the emotions he'd held for so long.

"I know," Maya whispered as tears flowed down her face. More than anyone - she did. She'd carried the same heavy burden.

Maya kept quiet, allowing Jesse to cry for as long as he needed. When Jesse could finally contain himself, she asked, "You okay?"

"I don't know. It's all so... I feel like I finally have a father, except now he's..." Jesse exhaled. "He asked me if I opened the envelope."

"What did you say?"

"Why are you crying, Mommy?" Benjamin asked as Maya opened the door to their apartment building.

"Mr. James passed away, buddy." Maya patted her son's head.

"He's with Jesus now."

Maya sniffled. "Yes, buddy. I think you're right."

Jesse seemed to get himself together enough to form a sentence. "I couldn't tell him. I didn't want him to know that he wasn't... I told him I didn't open it."

"It's okay, Jesse. Maybe it's better that way." Maya guided her son into the building.

"I couldn't do it."

Maya stepped inside the apartment building and guided her son to their front door. "It's okay, Jesse. You did the right—" Maya gasped. A bright yellow piece of paper was taped to their door.

"What's wrong?" Jesse asked.

"What's that, Mom?"

Maya pulled the paper down and stared at it. "An eviction notice."

"What!" Jesse asked.

"What's it for?" Benjamin asked in a much calmer voice, not knowing the seriousness of the situation.

"An eviction notice. We have thirty days to pack up and be out of the apartment." Her hands shook, rattling the page in her hand so hard she could hardly read it.

"We're moving?" Benjamin asked. "Cool."

"I'm coming over. Give me twenty minutes."

Before Maya could answer him, the elevator opened, and a man exited and approached, holding a large manila envelope.

"Maya Brown?" he asked.

"Yes." The word squeaked out as Maya's head swam.

"Please sign here." He pushed out a digital sign pad and Maya signed it. The man handed her the envelope and wished her a good day.

"What's that? What's going on?" Jesse asked.

"I don't know. Give me a second to get inside, and I'll open it."

"Go ahead and get settled. I'm on my way there now. You can tell me when I get there."

Maya agreed, ushered Benjamin inside, answering his questions as best as she could, and set him down at the table with a glass of milk and a plate of grapes. She sat in the chair across from him and set the envelope on the table.

Fearing that if she didn't open it now and get it over with she'd have a nervous breakdown, she slid open the top and pulled out a stack of papers that were nestled inside.

The top page was from Benjamin's school - Official discharge papers. Benjamin had been officially unenrolled from his private school.

Underneath that were pages and pages of itemized spreadsheets. Every single item Mrs. James had bought for them was listed, from the clothes on her son's back, the furniture they sat on, to the butter in their refrigerator.

Maya's body responded with shudders as she flipped through the continuing list.

26

JESSE

Jesse drove to his father's office in a rage. He'd told Maya he would be right there, but he needed to retrieve something first. He hoped that if what his father had told him was true, what he was looking for would be what he needed to fix the situation.

His mother had no plans to give in quietly, that was obvious. But with the information that his father had given him before he passed, Jesse was sure he could stop his mother's current rantings.

He'd misinterpreted the space his mother gave him to be with his father as an olive branch, but now, it was clear she'd only given him time so she could start the eviction process and whatever else she was cooking up.

For the life of him, Jesse couldn't understand his mother's need to control every situation. Everything had been settled. Jesse and his father had buried the hatchet, Benjamin had been all but welcomed into the family, and no one was making a big deal about the five years that were lost because of her. Still, she had an incessant need to make a splash. She was like a kid, eyeballing a puddle.

Jesse made it to the company building in record time, headed for his father's office, and went right for the same filing cabinet he and

Maya had looked through before. Underneath the file folders, right where his father said it would be, was an unmarked envelope. Jesse had no idea what he would find inside, but his father had said it would be everything he'd need in this event.

Jesse sat in his father's chair, which would now be his, and stared at the envelope. He never thought he would have to defend himself against his own mother, but it had obviously come to that and he wouldn't allow her to control one more aspect of his life.

His hand shook as he opened the envelope and pulled out a single page. After he unfolded it, he was surprised to find another police report. Only this one was a witness report written by one Claire James. He sped through the details. His mother claimed that she had come upon the scene, but Gloria Brown was already deceased.

"Why would she have been there?" The sound of his voice startled him in the silent room. "What was she visiting Maya's mother for?" And why wasn't this particular information in the folder with the rest of it?

"I only wanted to talk to her."

Jesse looked up to see his mother standing in the doorway. He hadn't even heard her coming this time.

"What did you do?"

"Your girlfriend Tina paid me a visit. She told me that Maya was pregnant and that she thought it might be yours. Of course I knew it was. The dates lined up and Maya didn't seem like the type of girl to sleep around."

"Tina is the one who told you Maya was pregnant? So what? You paid her a visit?"

"I only meant to speak to her mother."

"And."

"She knew who I was right away and invited me in."

Jesse waited for her to continue.

"Well, I told her that Maya was pregnant, and that I believed you were the father. I told her I wanted to take care of everything. I offered her the same deal I offered Maya."

"You bribed her mother?"

"It's not bribery, James. Don't be cocky. I was trying to protect Maya from your father."

"And from me?"

His mother looked away with a sniffle, but Jesse wasn't buying it. "From me, Mom? Did you ever stop to think that maybe I loved Maya? That maybe I wanted to be a father?"

"You left, Jesse!" His mother pointed a finger at him. "You abandoned us all and left me to pick up the pieces. I did the best I could."

"What did you do to her mother?"

His mother blew out a deep breath and sat in the chair across from him. "Get me a water."

Jesse leaned behind the desk and pulled a bottle of water from the refrigerator. He handed it to his mother and waited while she took a drink.

"I never meant for any of this to happen."

"What did you do?"

"She called me rich, racist, white trash! She said I was the reason people like her never got out of the ghetto. She said that Maya would never stoop so low as to have a relationship with my son, no matter how rich he was."

"Mom? What did you do?"

She covered her face. Her shoulders shook violently as she cried into her hands. Claire Brown was an expert at dramatizing her feelings to get what she wanted, but what Jesse was seeing looked genuine.

"Mom?" Jesse stood and came around the desk and leaned down in front of her, placing his hands on her knees. "What happened?"

His mother looked up, her blotchy face was streaked with mascara. "She pushed me and told me to get out. I don't know what exactly happened after that because everything happened so quickly."

"You pushed her back?"

His mother nodded her head.

"And then what?"

"She lost her balance. She fell and hit the coffee table. I ran toward her, but it was too late. She... Oh, Jesse, it was horrible. She gasped for air and the next thing I know, her body went still."

"And then you lied to the police?"

"I've been paying for it ever since! I took care of that girl and her son all these years because of the guilt."

"That girl is the girl I love, and that boy is my son. Your grandson. And now, since things didn't go the way you planned, you are having her evicted? Why, Mom?"

"That's not all."

Jesse stood and glared down at his mother, who refused to look him in the eyes. "What did you do?"

"What did you expect, Jesse? We had a contract, and she broke it!"

"What did you do?"

"I sent her the bill for everything I paid for her. And..."

"And?"

"I withdrew Benjamin from school."

"Mom! You're not making any sense! You brought me back here to take over the company. I am marrying Maya, which will make her just as much owner of the company as I am. Why would you do that?"

It made no sense to him. Even if he didn't plan to ask Maya to marry him, and if by chance she said no, Benjamin was still his son. He would never allow either of them to be homeless. His father had died, leaving him and his mother with billions of dollars.

"I don't know." She looked down at her hands. "I just wanted her to... to see all that I did for her. And for Benjamin. I love Benjamin, Jesse. He's my life now that your father is gone."

Jesse threw his hands in the air. "So this is some kind of scare tactic? Mom, I get that you don't like it when a situation is beyond your control, but you can't — "

"I know! I'm sorry! I don't know why — Jesse, my entire life just died. Your father is gone, and I feel like you are slipping away from me too. I just got you back."

"I have to go. Maya is frantic. I need to—"

"Are you going to tell her?"

"Tell her?"

"Don't make me say it."

"That you killed her mother? You think I should keep something like that away from her?"

His mother put her head back in her hands. "It was an accident."

"I'm going to tell her." Jesse picked up the paper and stormed to the door. "You better hope she shows more compassion on you than you have shown her."

Jesse left his mother sitting there with her head in her hands. Maybe being so harsh with her was not the right thing to do, but he didn't plan to keep anything from Maya. She had a right to know what happened to her mother, and Jesse wasn't about to live with the guilt of his mother's secret.

27

MAYA

Hours had passed, and Jesse still hadn't shown up. Maya and Benjamin had already picked up some boxes and Maya began going through her belongings, packing only what she would need.

If only I'd looked harder for a job. Thoughts of her bank account plagued her. While it held a significant amount of money, it wouldn't last for very long.

Maya studied her surroundings and ran a hand over her hair. While she wished she could count on Jesse to take care of everything, she couldn't help remembering it was because of him she and her son were facing this dilemma.

With each item she packed, she blamed Jesse more and more. She and Benjamin had been fine without him. They'd gotten by and Maya had learned to place all of her trust in God and pour out all of her love on Benjamin.

Maya grunted. From the moment she'd met Jesse, he'd caused her nothing but trouble. And where was he now? Once again, when she needed him, he was nowhere to be found.

"Why do we have to move?" Benjamin asked. "I like it here."

"I know, buddy. But we'll find another place. One just as good as this one."

"With my dad?"

Maya was shocked at his words but decided not to make a big deal out of it. "No. I don't think so."

"Why not?"

"Benjamin, I just don't know what's going on yet." What could she say? "Let's just close up these boxes for now and get some dinner."

"Okay." Benjamin shoved a couple toys in a box and closed it. "Can we order pizza?"

"Not today, buddy." Every cent would need to be saved for now on. The bottom line on the bill that Mrs. James gave her contained more zeros than she could count. In a matter of minutes, Maya had gone from being comfortably debt-free to swimming in bills. She could never pay Mrs. James back.

Her phone rang, and she picked it up from the counter, deciding that if it was Jesse, she would ignore it. She loved Jesse more than anyone in the world besides her own son, but dealing with him would leave her heartbroken again.

Hailey's picture popped up on the screen, and Maya's heart fell just a little. While she hadn't planned on answering Jesse — it would have been nice if he'd tried to call. Maya shook her head. He'd once again ditched her when she needed him most.

"Hey, Hailey." Maya tried to keep her voice level. "I'm a little busy right now. What's up?"

"I just thought you and Benjamin would like to meet me for pizza?"

"Yes!" Benjamin plopped down next to Maya.

"I guess he heard me?" Hailey laughed. "You want me to pick you up?"

"Yes. Sure." Maya gave in. She didn't feel like cooking, anyway. "Benjamin, run into my room and grab my shoes and purse." Maya wanted a moment to talk to Hailey alone.

Benjamin jumped up and ran from the room.

"She's evicting me," Maya whispered into the phone. "I don't know what to do."

"What? Who?"

"Mrs. James."

"Mo-om!" Benjamin called. "The black ones or the red ones?"

"Black ones, baby!" she called back.

"Mrs. James is evicting you? What are you going to do?"

"I don't know. Jesse was supposed to be here hours ago, but he never showed up."

"He won't let her do that."

"It looks like he has. For all I know, he's on a plane back to Guam."

"Come on." Hailey laughed. "That boy loves you more than sweet tea. He's not letting you go that easy."

Maya wiped a tear away as Benjamin came back into the room. "Thanks." She leaned down and slipped on her shoes. "You ready for some pizza, bud?" It was so hard to be upbeat for her son while their lives were caving in on them.

"Why don't you pack a couple of bags and come stay with me for a couple of nights. I'm sure this will all blow over, and Jesse will straighten everything out."

Maya wanted to believe her friend, but history had dictated something entirely different. "Yeah. I think that's a good idea. I could use the company."

"Okay. Pack a bag for you and Benjamin, and I'll be there in five."

Maya nodded and hung up, asking Benjamin to pack. As her son ran down the hall, she called, "Don't forget your underwear and toothbrush!"

It was then that Maya stood, realizing that she needed to use the restroom. She ran down the hall, the urge stronger than she realized. As she tried to unbutton and lower her pants, her phone slipped from her back pocket and plopped into the toilet.

"No!" Maya reached in and grabbed it just as it clicked to the bottom. "Why?"

Her eyes watered with frustration as she set it on a towel before sitting down to do her business. She stared at the black screen on her phone with a sigh.

After washing her hands, she started for her bedroom, threw her phone on the bed, and packed some clothes to take to Hailey's house. She'd never seen her friend's place, but wherever it was, it was better than being alone.

A horn honked outside, alerting Maya that Hailey was waiting, and Maya called out to Benjamin that it was time to leave. Throwing her water-logged phone into her purse, she grabbed her belongings, wondering when her life had become so crazy.

Maya and Benjamin piled into the taxi, and Maya told Hailey about her phone incident.

"Oh, don't worry about that. I've done that before. If you stick it in a bowl of rice for a couple of days, it will dry out inside and be as good as new."

"Thanks." Maya sighed with relief, hoping Hailey was right.

Maya glanced in her purse at her phone, longing to speak to Jesse. No matter how much she told herself she was better off without him, she couldn't see her future without Jesse in it.

It hurt more than a knife through the heart to walk away, but Maya had decided to never count on another soul to take care of her and Benjamin. That had been her first mistake.

"I need to look for a job right away."

"Ever think of driving? My company is always looking for drivers."

Maya wasn't too proud for any position. She'd flip burgers if it meant paying the bills for her and her son. "Sure. Where do I apply?"

The three of them ate pizza mostly in silence. Benjamin seemed to understand that something serious was taking place and kept to himself. Maya wanted to comfort him, but it was all she could do to force a slice of pizza down her throat and keep a smile on her face.

An hour later, they were back at Hailey's dinky, one-bedroom apartment. Maya had thought her apartment was small. Hailey's was less than half the size. A night or two would be fine, but Maya had no thoughts of staying any longer.

After Benjamin was ready for bed, Maya tucked him in on Hailey's couch and kissed his cheek. She prayed aloud just as they always did, asking God to bless everyone in their lives, including Jesse and Mrs. James. It was harder than ever to look at Benjamin and not fear for their future. She had to believe that God had everything under control. Hadn't she told Benjamin that so many times before? It was easy to say in times of ease, but at the moment, Maya found it hard to trust.

"Love you, buddy." Maya stood and tucked the surrounding blankets.

"I want to go home." His bottom lip protruded. "I don't like this blanket."

"I know. Just a couple of days while I try to sort everything out."

"Why don't you just call Mrs. James? She'll know what to do."

Maya's gut clenched. "Not this time, buddy." She wouldn't dare tell him that Mrs. James was the reason for their predicament.

Benjamin turned and covered his head, dismissing the conversation. He was much too young to have to deal with all of this.

28

JESSE

Three days had passed, and Jesse hunted for Maya high and low without success. When he'd arrived at her apartment, no one had answered. He'd thought maybe she'd just taken Benjamin out for some food, but after spending the entire night outside of her door, waiting, he realized she wasn't coming back.

Still, Jesse had gone to her apartment every day. He'd called her thousands of times, each time he ended up speaking to her voice-mail, begging her to call him back. He sent text upon text to her with no answer. Maya had seemed to have vanished from the earth — again.

Jesse's heart ached to speak to Maya. All he could imagine was that she was hurt or Benjamin was harmed. Where could she possibly go? Her mother had passed and her father, Maya had never really mentioned him.

Then it hit him — Hailey. She was the girl who had delivered the note for Maya. He'd tried to tell his mother that he and Hailey were dating, but obviously she had known all along that Jesse and Maya were seeing each other behind her back. They were friends. There was no way he would ever date one of Maya's friends.

Jesse pulled out his phone and searched local taxi companies in the area. As luck would have it, there were only two companies still running in the area. With many people using Uber or Lyft, taxi companies seemed to be in short supply. He dialed the first one and asked if they had a driver named Hailey. "Thin girl, light hair, blue eyes."

"Yes. Hailey works with us. Are you looking to be picked up?"

Jesse gave the dispatcher the location of a local grocery store, and the man promised to have her there in twenty to thirty minutes. Jesse jumped in his car and headed for the store. It was his last chance, and if Hailey saw him before he saw her, his plan might just be ruined. He guessed he finally understood the meaning of the words — not if I see you first.

Twenty minutes later, Jesse noticed the yellow cab pulling into the parking lot. Ducking behind the masonry, he waited for it to stop at the front door. It was her. He recognized her the second she pulled up.

When Jesse stepped into view, Hailey put the car in gear and punched the gas.

"Wait!" Jesse called. "Come on, Hailey! Please!"

When the car slowed, Jesse put his hands in the air, silently pleading with her. He breathed a sigh of relief when the taxi reversed and approached.

Once Hailey was close enough, she rolled down her window. "What do you want?"

"Where's Maya?"

"How should I know?" Hailey feigned innocence, but he could see she was lying.

"I just want to talk to her. Please, Hailey."

"I don't think she wants to talk to you."

"Is that why she's not answering her phone?"

Hailey smiled. "Actually, no. She dropped her phone in the, uh, water. We put it in rice, but it never came to."

"Maybe you could just give her a message for me?" Jesse pleaded with his eyes.

"Fine. Make it quick but I can't guarantee you she will read it. She's pretty upset after you ditched her."

"I didn't… just give her the message to call me." He didn't have time to explain that his mother had waylaid him for half the night while she tried to convince him she hadn't meant to murder another human being.

"Maybe you should write your number?" Hailey asked. "I mean, she might have stored it in her phone, but maybe she didn't commit it to memory?"

"Yeah." Jesse rattled off his number, while Hailey entered it into her phone. "Maybe you could let me know when she gets the message?"

"Do I have a choice?"

"What do you mean?"

"Am I going to have to fear every time I get a call from dispatch to pick up a rider at a grocery store?"

Jesse tilted his chin. "I'll switch it up. You'll never know where I might call from next."

Hailey rolled her eyes. "I'll give her the message, and I'll text you after I do. That's the best I can do."

"Thanks, Hailey." Jesse stepped back. "Where's she staying, anyway?"

"Good try, rich boy." Hailey winked and shoved the car into gear, her tires squealing.

"It was worth a try." For a moment, Jesse almost followed Hailey to see where she led him, but he quickly decided against anything that would put him in the stalker category. He would just have to trust Maya to call him. Maya could be stubborn, but she was smart. Even if he was wrong and she didn't love him, she would do the right thing where their son was concerned.

29

───────

MAYA

It had been three long days of applying for job after job. Maya clicked on so many sites her eyes were almost permanently crossed. The good news was that she'd downloaded her resume to dozens of companies and had several interviews lined up for the next week. All that was left was to convince one of them to give her a job.

"When am I going back to school?" Benjamin asked for the millionth time.

"We'll enroll you in a new school tomorrow," Maya said without looking at her son who had flopped down on the couch next to her.

"But I like my old school. All my friends are there."

"I'm sorry, buddy. Maybe next year I will be able to afford to get you back in. For now, we are all going to have to make concessions."

This was exactly why she'd not wanted to allow Mrs. James to spoil him. He had no idea what it meant to make concessions. He was used to getting what he wanted a good deal of the time, and although Maya wasn't against a child learning the value of money, she didn't think she would have to be teaching him that lesson so soon.

"Do I get to go with Mrs. James this weekend?"

"I thought you and I would hang out with Hailey and binge watch some superhero movies."

"But I always go with Mrs. James on Saturday," he whined.

"Not this week, buddy. I'm sorry."

"But, Mom—"

"Benjamin!" Maya stood, almost dropping her laptop. "I said you are staying home this weekend. I don't want to hear another word about it!"

Benjamin's face fell. "Sorry." His eyes glistened with tears, and he turned away.

Maya felt like the worst mother on the planet. She was a failure. Without Mrs. James providing everything for them, Maya had no ability to parent her child. If she were honest with herself, she'd done very little of the things parents did for their children. She hadn't provided stability or even paid for his basic needs. Mrs. James had done all of that. The only thing Maya had contributed was love. Love was a powerful motivator, but there was much more needed than that to care for a child.

"Come here, buddy. Mommy is really stressed right now. I'm sorry for yelling at you."

Benjamin fell into her lap and wrapped his arms around her. "It's okay. You're still a good mom." How her son knew she needed to hear those words was beyond her, but as soon as they left his mouth, they touched her heart. She could do this. She could provide for her and her son. She didn't need Jesse or Mrs. James. She would do it on her own.

"Thanks, buddy." Maya kissed the top of her son's head. "You're a pretty good kid yourself."

"I don't really like none of those kids, anyway. Doyle's a stupid head, and he tries to get the other kids to be mean to me sometimes."

This was the first Maya had heard of anyone being mean to him, but it didn't surprise her. Maya went to school with many of his peers parents. They were mostly all stuck up and full of themselves. She guessed they were teaching their children to hate at a young age.

The front door opened and Hailey came through holding a couple of bags from the local Chinese restaurant. "Anyone want Orange Chicken?"

"I do!" Benjamin ran to the table. "And sticky rice!"

"Easy to please." Maya smiled. "How was your day?"

Hailey set the food on the table, while Maya grabbed paper plates and plasticware for their food. As it turned out, Hailey didn't wash many dishes. Most of her eatery items were throwaway. "Makes life easier when you live on the run," she'd said.

Maya didn't bother mentioning how many landfills it took to dispose of all that extra waste. She was happy to be there instead of alone in her apartment, where every single item reminded her of Mrs. James, and in turn, Jesse.

Hailey dished out a scoop of chicken for Benjamin and then some rice. "So, I had an interesting customer today."

"Yeah?" Maya scooped out a small amount of chicken. "Interesting how?"

"Well, I got a call from dispatch to pick up a guy at Fry's. Tall, military looking guy."

Maya looked up.

"Rich, white, buzz cut, has a mother who—"

"You gave Jesse a ride?" The thought of Jesse taking a cab anywhere was ridiculous. Mr. James had more vehicles than a new car dealership. There was no reason for Jesse to take a taxi.

"Yup. Only he didn't really want a ride. He had a message to deliver."

Maya gritted her teeth until they hurt. When had her life become so confusing? After three days of sleeping on one end of a couch while her son kicked and rolled, keeping her up all night, Maya was ready to give in. She'd not had one instance of privacy and she just wanted to go back home. It wasn't much, but it was her home. Regardless of how she felt about Jesse, he was the only one who could help her out of her current situation. He was the only person who could turn everything around and make things right again.

"What's the message?"

"He just asked you to call him." Hailey handed Maya a ripped half of a grocery receipt. "His number is on the back."

Maya had committed Jesse's number to memory. It didn't matter that her phone had never survived the water-boarding it received. "That's it? Just call him? What if it's a trap?"

A laugh bubbled from Hailey. "Girl, are you blind or are you seriously that dumb?"

"Hailey!" Maya looked over at Benjamin, who was paying too much attention to his orange chicken to notice.

"Oh." Hailey covered her mouth. "You know what I mean."

"Yeah, Mom." Benjamin agreed. "Are you blind or what?"

"Benjamin!" So much for him not paying attention.

"What?" Benjamin shoved a fork of rice into his mouth. "He likes you and he is my dad. What's so bad about that?"

"It's just not that easy, bud." There were so many things that a five-year-old could never understand, and Maya didn't feel like trying to explain to anyone why the thought of trying to work things out with Jesse made her stomach turn and twist in all directions.

"Well, I like him even if you don't!" Benjamin dropped his fork onto his paper plate, stood, and stormed out of the room.

Maya watched him leave but didn't follow him. Hailey's place was too small for him to go too far, and Maya needed a second to figure out how she would explain it all to him.

"Sorry." Hailey looked down at her food. "Guess I overstepped."

"What do I do?"

Hailey stood and took the seat next to Maya. Touching her arm, she said, "What's going on? I know you like him." She smiled. "And he likes you, too. What's so hard about letting him in?"

Maya looked back at Benjamin, who was pouting on the couch. "It's just that — I guess our history is too — It's Jesse. He's—"

"He's in love with you, Maya. I don't know how you can't see it, but if I were you, I wouldn't let this one go."

Maya wiped at her eyes as tears misted in them. "You don't understand, Hailey. I just don't know if we can—"

"Jeremy Thompson." Hailey's eyes seemed far away. "We dated for four years. My father hated him."

"What happened?"

"My father hated him," she repeated as if that made all the sense in the world.

"And?"

"How could I disappoint my father?" Hailey wrung her hands.

"So, you stopped dating him because of your father?"

"No. He stopped dating me. It was my fault. I would never stick up for him. I wanted our relationship to be a secret yet I still wanted to date him."

"You just didn't want your father to know?"

"Yeah. Only that backfired on me. He got tired of pretending we weren't together. Look, Maya. All I'm saying is — life is too short to worry about pleasing others. If you care about Jesse, you should see if you can make it work. Benjamin deserves to have a father in his life, and you deserve to be happy."

"If only life were that simple."

"If only." Hailey sighed.

"What happened to Jeremy?" Maya gave Hailey a sad smile.

"He still lives here. He's married now with a kid."

"Do you ever see him? Is it hard?" The thought of living in the same town as Jesse and seeing him with another woman, or not, pained her. Jesse wouldn't wait forever for her to make up her mind.

"I see him every now and then. It's… yeah, it hurts."

"I'm sorry." Maya touched her as Hailey wiped the tears from her own face.

"This is the life of Hailey." She pointed to herself. "Sad, alone, living in a tiny apartment, driving a taxi. Don't be like Hailey."

"Oh, stop it." Maya patted her friend on the knee. "You've got plenty going for you. One day you'll meet a guy that knocks you off your feet and you won't even remember Jeremy."

Hailey gave Maya a sad smile. "If I told you those same words about Jesse, how would you respond?"

"I can't imagine ever loving anyone more than I love Jesse."

Hailey reached over and took the crinkled grocery receipt from Maya's sweaty hands. She unfolded it, smoothed it out, and handed it back. "Call him."

Maya nodded, staring down at the numbers on the page. "Yeah. Okay. I better talk to Benjamin first."

"Good girl."

Maya moved to the living room and sat down next to her son. "Hey, buddy." She placed an arm around her son's shoulders.

"It's just not fair." Benjamin looked up at his mother, his doe eyes glossy with unshed tears.

"What's not fair?"

"Doyle has a dad. Carter has a dad. Even Emily has a dad. She only sees him on the weekend, but he does fun things with her."

"And you want a dad, too?"

Benjamin nodded.

"You know that no matter what happens between me and your father, he will always be your dad, right?"

"Why don't you like him?"

"Oh, baby." Maya pulled him close. "I do. I like him very much. Things are just kind of complicated right now."

"Is Mrs. James really his mom? She's nice too. She always buys me things and tells me she loves me."

"Yes, she is. And she does love you so much."

"Then why did she make us leave our house? And my school with my friends and everything?"

"It's really complicated, buddy, but I will try to explain it to you since you are such a big boy."

Benjamin nodded.

"A long time ago, when you were still in my tummy, Mrs. James and I made a deal. She promised to take care of us both as long as I kept you a secret."

"A secret?"

"Yep. And she kept her word. She took such good care of you. And she does love you, Benjamin. So much." No matter what Mrs. James had done, she had kept her word and Maya was grateful.

"From who?"

Maya swallowed. This was the hardest part of her story, and maybe Benjamin was too young to hear it, but she'd already gone too far to turn back now. "Your grandfather and dad."

Benjamin watched his mother carefully as recognition played in his eyes. "Oh." Tears spilled from his eyelids down his cheeks. "That's not very nice."

"No, it's not, but Mrs. James was trying to protect you."

"Oh." He wiped his eyes. "From who?"

It was obvious that Benjamin was too young to understand. "It's complicated, buddy, but Mrs. James thought she was doing the right thing."

Not satisfied with his mother's answer, Benjamin threw his arms over his chest. "From Mr. James, huh?"

Maya looked back at Hailey, who still sat at the small kitchen table. Hailey poked her bottom lip out and shrugged. She would be no help.

"One day, when you're older, I'll explain it to you. I just need you to know that she thought what she was doing was right." Mrs. James had been protecting Jesse, not Benjamin. She knew, or at least thought she did, that Mr. James would cut Jesse from the company if he found out that the two of them had brought a child into the world. Mrs. James' best option was to quietly take care of Jesse's offspring with no one knowing the truth. That plan had backfired.

"I'm not hungry anymore. Can I get ready for bed?"

Maya looked at the clock. It was still early, but she didn't have the heart to push him anymore. "Sure. Let's get you in your pajamas. We are registering you for a new school in the morning."

30

———

JESSE

Jesse stared at the paperwork laid in front of him. His mother had done it. It wasn't official, but the request had been submitted for Jesse to receive an honorable early discharge. His command master chief had granted him three months terminal leave, which was all the time he had on the books and plenty of time for the documentation to come back pardoning him of any further service.

He wasn't exactly sure how he felt about it. He'd made a life in the military, and he'd been his own man. But his father was gone. They'd given him a beautiful service and laid him to rest. It was time for Jesse to take over the family business. He hoped and prayed that Maya would be a part of it, but even if she didn't, Jesse was ready to step up and make his father proud. Besides, Maya's rejection didn't make Jesse any less of a father. He had every intention to be in his son's life. That he would fight for if he had to.

His phone rang with an unknown number and Jesse stared at it, wondering whether he should answer or not. As a general rule, he didn't answer numbers he didn't recognize, but he wouldn't dare miss a single call just in case it was Maya.

"Hello?" Jesse answered.

"Hi."

"Maya?"

"It's me." Her voice was soft, quiet.

"Hey. Are you okay?"

"Hailey told me you wanted me to call?"

"I need to see you. I have so much to tell you… and ask you… Can we meet?"

"What are we doing?" Her voice sounded desperate, breaking his heart.

"What do you mean?" Jesse held his breath, waiting for what he already knew. She was scared and his family had made her that way.

"Why are we trying to beat the odds, Jesse? Maybe we just weren't meant to be."

"Maya, I was coming to see you. I was on my way there, but I had to go to my father's office first. There was something he wanted me to get. He knew we would need it."

"What?"

"I can't tell you over the phone. I need to see you."

"I don't know. This is so hard on Benjamin. He's so confused."

"Give me half an hour." Jesse closed his eyes. "Hear me out, and if you still hate me after that, you can … well," Jesse smiled. "You can never get rid of me, Maya. I want to be in my son's life. And I want to be in yours too."

Maya gave a sigh that Jesse recognized as defeat. "Fine. Thirty minutes."

"Good. Give me the address."

Maya rattled off the address, and Jesse jumped into his rental. Although his mother had spoken little to him since their last conversation, he was sure he had access to whatever vehicle he wanted, but he wasn't ready to let his mother off the hook yet. He'd decided that whatever happened would be one-hundred percent Maya's decision. Even if it meant they tried his mother for murder.

Fifteen minutes later, Jesse pulled up to a small apartment complex not far from where Maya lived. He glanced down at the scrap of paper he'd scribbled the address on and went to apartment five. He knocked on the door and waited only a second before Hailey answered.

"There's my boyfriend." Hailey winked at him. "Come on in."

Jesse's face reddened at the lie he'd told his mother about him and Hailey. "Yeah. No one believes that story."

"Bummer." Hailey laughed. "Come on. Maya's in the kitchen."

Jesse headed toward the kitchen but stopped when he saw Benjamin sleeping on the couch. Pressing back the urge to pick the little guy up and hold him in his arms, Jesse followed Hailey to the kitchen. Soon, he would have all the time in the world to get to know his son. No matter what the outcome with Maya, he would do all he could to be in his son's life. Nothing or no one would stop him. He just hoped Maya saw how much he loved them both. The thought of being in Benjamin's life and seeing Maya only where it concerned their son was like bullet holes in his gut. He wanted the three of them to be a family.

From the moment he saw her sitting at the kitchen table, he knew he didn't want to live life one more second without her.

Maya looked up. "Hey." She gave him that same fake smile as she did when they were teenagers and she was having a bad day.

Jesse sat down across from her. "Hey."

"You wanted to talk?"

"This is going to be the hardest conversation I've ever had."

Maya set her hands on the table and folded them together. "You have twenty-nine minutes."

"Not giving me any breaks, are ya?"

"Jesse, just say what you have to say, please. Whatever it is, we need to settle this now. I just can't—"

"I never meant for any of this to happen. I'm sorry my family is so messed up and—"

"Racist?"

Jesse frowned. "To be fair, that's just my father. He had some old-fashioned ideas about—" Jesse wasn't willing to make anymore excuses for his father. "Yeah. Racist."

"It's fine. He's gone. And besides, he wasn't so bad."

"Did you see the way his eyes lit up when he saw Benjamin?"

Jesse smiled despite himself. "I think he would have been okay with everything." If only his mother hadn't tried to control every situation. "There's more, though. You were right."

"About what?"

"I don't know how to say this." Jesse looked away. He had to get it out of the way before he could ask her his pending question. How she took this information could either crush their relationship or strengthen it. "Remember those papers we found in my dad's office? The one about your mother's death?"

Maya nodded.

Jesse pulled the folded up police report from his pocket and unfolded it. He handed it to her.

"What is this?"

"Read it." Jesse nodded.

Maya scanned the page. "Another police report?"

Jesse nodded for her to continue. Maya read through it and then looked up. "What does this mean? I don't understand."

"Who's name is on that report?" Jesse prodded.

Maya's eyes searched the page until they settled on the name. "Your mom? She called the police? Why would she have been at my house?"

Jesse explained the story to Maya just as his mother had told him. It broke his heart to tell her, but he needed to be completely honest from here on out. There was no way they could start again with another hidden secret.

"It was an accident. She heard about the pregnancy, and she went to confront your mother about it. I guess your mother didn't know yet. They argued and…"

"It was an accident," Maya whispered as she stared at a spot on the wall. "It was an accident."

"I'm sorry, Maya. I'm willing to do whatever you want about it. We can call the police right now if that's what you want. We'll file a report. Whatever."

"It was an accident?"

Jesse nodded. With each repeat of the same four words, he worried Maya was going into some kind of shock. "If it's any consolation, my mother has agreed to forgive your debt entirely. She understands what she's done and even if you press charges, she still wishes to forgive you of your debt."

"It was an accident."

"Maya, I wish you would say something. I mean, something else. You're scaring me."

Maya looked at him plainly. "I just… I'm so confused." Maya averted her eyes. "I remember that day so clearly. I was showing more and more. The kids at school had already caught on and had been harassing me for a while. I decided I was going to tell my mom before she noticed on her own. I never… I was so scared to tell her and then when she… I'm so ashamed of myself." Maya dropped her head into her hands.

"What? Maya, why?"

She looked up, sadness etched into her eyes. "I was so afraid to tell her I was pregnant. My mom had big plans for me. She wanted me to become a doctor. She couldn't wait until I did. She said she was going to quit working and let me take care of her. My mom worked so hard." Maya wiped her eyes. "And that day…" Maya dropped her head back into her hands.

"What's wrong? What happened?"

"All day long I prayed for something to happen so that I didn't have to tell my mother I was pregnant. I couldn't bear to disappoint her."

"Oh, honey." Jesse stood and brought Maya into his arms. "This isn't your fault. You know God didn't strike your mother down because you asked for a way out of this, right?"

"I know!" Maya huffed. "But back then, even though everyone said it was stupid, I was sure it was my fault!"

"No." Jesse held her tight. "It wasn't your fault." Guilt held him so tightly that he felt as though he might stop breathing. This was his fault. If only he'd have fought for her from the very beginning instead of running, everything would be different.

Maya wiped away a tear that slid down her face. "What do we do?"

This was his moment. Everything he'd ever wanted would count on how she responded to his one simple question. Getting down on his knee, Jesse pulled the box from his pocket. His body shook with the fear of rejection.

Maya placed a hand over her mouth and shook her head. "No, Jesse. Please." She closed her eyes.

"I can't, Maya. I can't take one more day without you. Please. I need you. I love you. Maybe you don't love me like I have always loved you, but—"

"I do. We just can't. There's too much past. Too much baggage. It will never work between us."

"Says who?"

"The odds are against us. We just… can't."

Jesse looked down at the ring still sparkling in his hand. Closing the box, he got back to his feet. "We missed this opportunity before, and that was on me. When I left town, I didn't know I was leaving Benjamin, but I knew I was leaving the only girl I would ever love. It was cowardice of me, and if I could go back and do things differently, I swear to you, I would do it. I would have stayed. I'd have stood up to my father and mother even if it cost me my inheritance. There is no amount of money in the world that's worth losing the only thing that makes you smile in the morning." Jesse wiped at the tears that threatened to fall. "That's right. I hadn't truly smiled in years before I came back home and saw you." He pointed to the living room. "And that little guy in there… Praise God that he forgives me because I will never forgive myself for missing five years of his life."

"I want to believe it can work."

Jesse took Maya's hands in his and pulled her to him. "Do you love me?"

Maya nodded.

"Do you trust me?"

Maya grinned.

"Oh, come on! I was a teenager!"

"You were a rotten teenager."

"I was. But luckily for me, I figured out this adulting thing pretty successfully."

Maya raised an eyebrow. "What do we do about your mother?"

"Is that a yes?"

"Was there a question?"

Jesse got back down on his knees, took the ring from the box and held it out. "Maya Brown, will you marry me?"

"Yes." Maya held out her hand.

Jesse took her hand in his and slipped the ring on her finger. "I promise to make you the happiest woman alive."

Maya smiled, making his heart swell with love. "You got a lot of making up to do."

"I do. To you and Benjamin."

EPILOGUE

Maya sat at the same desk she'd been sitting for the last five years, only this time it was for her fiance, not her father-in-law, and there were no secrets. In a few months, Maya would officially be Mrs. Jesse James and she had no regrets.

After a long conversation with Jesse's mom, Maya found it in her heart to forgive the woman for the death of her mother. Mrs. James was a manipulator and a control freak, but she was no killer. Whatever had transpired between them, Maya believed Mrs. James had not meant to do her mother harm. Besides, Benjamin loved her, and she couldn't see taking another grandmother away from him.

"Do you really trust her?" Hailey, who was sitting across from Maya, poking pens into the rocks in the jar on Maya's desk, asked.

"What do you mean?" Maya looked up.

"You know," Hailey cocked her head as if there was someone listening. "Mrs. James."

"Not as far as I can throw her." Maya grinned.

"But you said you forgave her." Hailey gave her a sceptical look. "Isn't that the Christian way?"

"Yes, I forgave her. But that doesn't mean I have to trust her."

"I'll never understand you Christians." Hailey shook her head.

Maya smiled. Hailey was on her way, and she didn't even know it.

"Well, who do we have here?" Jesse said, popping his head in the doorway.

"Your fiance and your girlfriend," Hailey teased. "I thought I'd take Maya out to lunch and tell her about my new job."

"What new job?" Maya asked, turning to face her friend.

"Girl, you will never believe what happened." Hailey stood. "I got a job at a detective agency."

ENJOYED THIS BOOK? YOU CAN MAKE A DIFFERENCE.

Do reviews intimidate you? Don't know exactly what to say? There is no right or wrong. As a reader, you have amazing influential power in helping others decide which books to read. If you enjoyed my words … please take a minute to write a few of your own and let others know.

To leave a review of – The Billionaire's UnWelcome Home –click here[1]

Thank you very much!

---

1. https:www.amazon.com/dp/B07PKS1H85

SNEAK PEEK - INVESTIGATING THE RANCHER
CHAPTER 1 - HAILEY

Hailey Baker looked intently into her bathroom mirror, crinkled her nose, and rolled her eyes. Why was it that no matter how long she'd been applying her makeup, she still managed to get one eyebrow looking lower than the other?

It was her lot in life, but the least of her worries. Since she'd come back home to the family business and the — family, Hailey had been on edge.

No matter how many times she told herself it was the right thing to do, she missed the other, short-lived, yet wonderfully peaceful life she'd experienced in between this annoying one. The one where no one judged her, and no one gave her endless advice.

Her best friend, Maya, had been there, the only one she'd ever been able to talk to, yet Hailey had kept her entire life a secret. That was the baggage of a taxi driver. They carried the burden of listening to everyone else's problems, but never expressed their own. It was okay, though. She'd left to get away from her problems, not spread them all about.

Besides, Maya was instrumental in bringing Hailey to an acceptance of her life and ultimately to God. It was crazy how a brief moment in a person's life changed their outlook completely. Maya was busy in her new life now, but she'd left Hailey with the everlasting gift of grace. Something she well needed these days.

With a grunt of frustration, she whipped out a cotton ball from her Kaboodle and dabbed at the penciled-in eyebrow. Being that she was fair-skinned with hair somewhere between light and very-light, depending on the time of year, her brows were barely visible. "Au-natural it is."

It didn't matter, anyway. She wouldn't be seeing her boyfriend, Rob, for an entire week since he'd be traveling out of town in a matter of hours. Who else was there to look good for? Her father, who was still so wrapped up in the mysterious disappearance of their mother over a decade ago that he couldn't think straight? Or her sister, Melody, who hated Hailey because she'd wrecked her teenage years by being forced to suffer through the role of mother and sibling at the same time?

After the disappearance of their mom, when Hailey was eight and her sister was twelve, their father had forced Melody to drag Hailey around everywhere she went. Hailey had even accompanied Melody on dates when their dad was away on one investigation or another, and he deemed Hailey too immature to remain home alone.

Melody acted as if it was a delight for Hailey to be dragged all over town, making her observe her sister's make-out sessions with her boyfriend-of-the-week. Not that her sister was promiscuous. Hailey was fairly certain that at twenty-seven, Melody was still as pure as snow. Another reason she was better than Hailey, who wouldn't recognize love if it smacked her on the lips.

But this time, Hailey had gotten it right, and there was nothing Melody could say about it. Rob was a wonderful guy, and although he was two years older than Hailey and had been her high school crush, first kiss, and other regretful firsts, they were both much more mature now.

When Hailey came into her womanhood, so to speak, Melody's boyfriends started giving Hailey second glances. Their attention had been another huge contention between Melody and Hailey. No sixteen-year-old girl wanted her boyfriend ogling her twelve-year-old sister.

Enter Rob. They met at a party in Hailey's senior year of high school. As far as she'd known, Rob and Melody had never even met. Rob was living in an altogether different world than Melody. Yet when Hailey had finally mustered up the nerve to introduce them, the room had become uncomfortably silent.

Hailey never did figure out what was going on there, but she knew that something had transpired between them. Truthfully, she didn't care. Melody had always treated her like chopped liver, and Hailey was tired of trying to meet her sister's outrageous standards.

With all that had happened over the years, she was confident that Melody had thrown a celebration the day Hailey walked out on the family investigating business to pursue a career in taxi driving.

Hailey's stomach knotted at the way the actions of their mother had crushed her relationship with her own flesh-and-blood sister. And her father… that was a story for another time.

A thought occurred to her as she tried one more time to apply her eyebrow pencil with a little more finesse. "I'll just stop by and bring Rob a coffee before he leaves for his flight." She smiled, admiring her second attempt at twin arching eyebrows. Two almost perfectly shaped cornucopias smiled back at her.

"You go, girl!"

Rob being on business for the entire coming week made her want to cry. Without him, she was surrounded by nutzos. For an entire week, she would have to listen to her father explain how he might have a lead on their mother's disappearance, while her sister eyeballed her and made rude comments about Hailey's inability to act responsibly in any given situation.

So, yeah. Hailey had gone through a rougher teenage rebellion than the norm, but that was just how it was. She'd held in a lot of anger over her mother's abandonment. Melody should have been the first one to understand that, but she'd been the hardest one on Hailey. It was her constant disapproving looks, critical opinions, and controlling attitude that had sent Hailey off, reeling at the world for all of its unfairness. And then Rob popped back into her life, messaging her on Facebook, blowing up her phone, and Face-timing her daily, begging her to forget the past and come back home.

And here she was. . .

Without another thought for her family, Hailey grabbed her purse and rushed out of her apartment. If she timed it just right, she would be there to wake him with a fresh cup of coffee. That made her smile. He was the one good point in her life. It was Rob, her old high school boyfriend who found her on social media and had convinced her to come back home and give *Baker and Sons Investigative Services* another chance.

There were no sons. Noah Baker had started his investigative services just after he and their mother married. Originally, her father named the company *Baker Investigations*, but when their mom got pregnant with Melody, they were sure it would be a boy. What a disappointment it must have been for her dad after buying the copyright for the name and then never having a son. Now, the name was more of a conversation piece than anything else, but sometimes Hailey wondered if her dad wasn't disappointed to have girls instead of boys.

The moment the cold air hit her, Hailey was instantly reminded that she was no longer living in Trust, Arizona, where the extreme heat temperatures ran up into the triple digits. In her hometown of Snowflake, the weather reached a warm eighty in the middle of summer. Hailey ran back in and grabbed the fur-lined jacket she'd tossed onto the couch the night before.

"Brr." Her breath steamed through the air, bringing back memories better left in the past. Rubbing her arms, Hailey got the distinct feeling she should turn around and go back to bed.

"Nope. You've got work today." Small in the encouragement department, but it was the best she could do. "Daddy don't pay slouches." Her father was a stickler about his daughter's earning their own way. If she didn't make rent, she'd be sleeping back at his house. That was not an option. She'd go crazy if she had to live in that den of memories again. Jumping in her little blue Eclipse, she blasted her heat and headed for Rob's house.

Twelve minutes later, Hailey was at Rob's apartment door. With a steaming hot cup of coffee in one hand, and a last-minute donut in the other, she struggled to nudge the carpet sideways enough for his spare key to come into view. She'd used it several times to enter his apartment to feed and walk his Doberman, Ruby, for him when he was away on business trips.

Looking down, she examined the situation. With her purse over one arm, a coffee in one hand and a donut bag in the other, something was bound to go wrong when she bent over to get the key. Shoving the donut bag in her purse, she reached down, grabbed the key without her purse strap sliding down her arm, and stood, key in hand, with perfect precision. Slipping it into the front door, she opened it carefully and quietly so as not to wake him yet.

Inside, Rob's normally messy apartment was eerily clean. Not only were all the fast-food bags and soda cans cleared away from the coffee table, but his living room carpet had the distinct markings of a vacuum cleaner being run over top of it. No one would accuse Rob of being a neat-freak, and he usually went to great lengths to be sure of that.

Hailey had cleaned his apartment on more than one occasion. But not recently.

Hailey glanced back at the carpet. Did Rob even know how to use his vacuum?

A movement caught her eye, startling her for a split second before realizing that Ruby had not met her at the door like she normally did.

Hailey turned. Sure enough, Ruby was on the back porch, her breath making puffs of fog on the sliding glass door. As soon as they made eye contact, Ruby slapped her paw onto the glass and whined. Hailey headed in Ruby's direction but stopped dead in her tracks when a moan arose from the area of the back bedroom.

Her first thought was that Rob was in pain, but as her legs carried her into that direction, the moans grew heavier, more distinct ... and they were not coming from just one person.

Anger steamed from Hailey's face and neck, making sweat beads form. Her mind ran in all directions, knowing very well what she was hearing, yet not wanting to believe it. Her first instinct was to turn around, go back to the front door, and leave without him ever knowing she'd been there. Turning on her heels, she glanced back at Ruby, who was now scratching at the door latch to get in.

She could let Ruby in and Rob would know that she'd been there, or at least that someone had. But she needed proof. As demented as it was, Hailey needed to see what was going on back there with her own eyes.

She continued down the hall. With each step, the sound effects grew louder. When she reached the door, she turned the handle without caring to ponder what she might see on the other side. If she thought too much about it, she'd walk out the door, and he'd explain it away as if it were nothing… just like he did back then…

She'd fallen for his lies again, and that was too much disappointment for Hailey to handle. Touching the cold door handle, her nerves twisted, her stomach bunched into tiny knots. Fearing she'd never get the scene out of her head, she took a step back. Another set of moans flowed through the door and her ire flared. She was too angry to turn back now.

Turning the handle, Hailey whipped open the door with the wild force driven by her anger alone. It slammed into the spring door stopper, then bounced back, almost into her face. The door stopper boinged through the chilly air, grabbing the attention of all.

Rob jumped out of his bed, stark naked, and snatched the sheet, pulling it around him, leaving the woman fully exposed.

"Robby!" the woman called, pulling at the sheet he was hogging to cover his own shame. Completely exposed, her eyes were as big as watermelons as she stared at Hailey. "What's going on? Who is she?"

Rob stared wide-eyed back and forth between the two of them. The woman leaned down and struggled to get the fitted sheet that wouldn't let go of its hold on the bed, and Hailey staring at the scene, unable to look away.

"Hailey? What are you doing here?"

"I… I… brought you coffee." Hailey held out the cup as if she were the one caught cheating.

"*You* brought *him* coffee?" The woman grabbed an edge of the sheet from Rob and snatched it away, leaving him to struggle for his clothes. "My husband? You brought coffee for my husband? I suppose you let yourself in with your own key too?" She turned back to Rob. "Looks like some things never change!"

With a whirl, the woman was next to Hailey. Plucking the cup from her hands, the woman snapped the top off and shoved it forward. Then, as if in slow motion, coffee streamed through the air, landing directly on the cheating scoundrel. Hailey's hand flew to her mouth in horror as Rob writhed in pain.

"That's what you get, you filthy… ugh!" Tears moistened the woman's face as she struggled to get her underclothes on without being exposed.

Rob backed into the master bathroom, still in obvious pain, and closed the door. Hailey didn't believe in violence, but this time, the punishment seemed to fit the crime. He'd burned them both, and if it left a scar, maybe it would be a reminder in future endeavors. Not with her. She was done with him. But even a jerk like him could learn from something. Or was that too much to hope?

"I'm sorry," Hailey whispered. Without a moment's notice, Hailey had turned from victim to violator. "I had no idea."

The woman shook her head as she slipped her pants on. "Don't worry about it, honey. I didn't marry you. I married him." She sneered at the bathroom door and then shouted, "And I'm glad I found out he hasn't changed one bit since we decided to try to reconcile our marriage."

"I'm glad I found out too." Hailey glared at the door, glad she didn't have to see his cheating face. "Now I don't have to waste another second of my time."

Feeling like a complete idiot for thinking Rob could have changed, Hailey flipped around and stormed out. Her face steamed with anger and embarrassment, her eyes filling with tears. She'd trusted him, and he'd let her down. For all she'd had to endure since being back, she could have stayed in that quiet little town of Trust and continued to drive her taxi.

She'd made friends there. Maya, her closest one, came to mind. She'd shared more with the girl than anyone else. Maya had seen her share of hardships, and she'd never judged Hailey. But Maya was living her own life now with her husband and their son. If Hailey wasn't feeling as if she were drowning, she'd dare to wish she too could have a happy ending.

If it weren't for Rob, she'd still be there, completely unaware of the pain she was now feeling. Why? As she jumped into her car, it was the only question that came to mind. Why did he do this to me? He has a wife! And then — How could I not have known?

Now, she was stuck working for her father. She'd sold her taxi and bought her little two door Eclipse that was too small to even work for Uber or Lift. No one wanted to climb in and out of the back bucket seats, smashing their heads on the door frame, as they bent their legs awkwardly to get in and out. At a short five-three, even she had trouble getting in and out of the back seat when she had to.

Kicking herself as she stared out the window, she wiped her eyes, took a deep breath, and sighed. Humming a tune to keep her mind off the situation she'd just walked into, she concentrated on the day ahead. Rob was none of her business anymore.

But guilt and questions still plagued her mind. Obviously Rob's wife had not lived there in the house with him. Hailey had been inside it frequently with no sign of a woman's touch or anything to indicate one had been there. The woman did mention they were trying to reconcile, so maybe she wasn't even from there. Did she fly in from another state? Maybe she lived in the Phoenix area?

It didn't matter. Although Hailey would have loved to hear the full story about her childhood sweetheart and his unmentioned failing marriage, she wasn't willing to stay in that house one second longer. It was their story to sort out, and she was only an interference. Still, it bit her she'd fallen for the guy a second time. He'd burned her once back in high school, and now he'd gotten her again. The vision of hot coffee flying through the air, hitting Rob square in the chest, made her cringe.

"Lord, forgive me." Starting the car, she headed back to her father's office. She'd never wished anyone so much anguish as she did Rob. "Vengeance is Yours, not mine." She hadn't thrown the coffee, but she'd gained too much satisfaction from it to be healthy. She wouldn't allow a jerk like Rob to nestle inside her heart and damage it. It was already broken enough.

Before Hailey realized it, she was back in the driveway of Baker and Sons Investigative Services. The building was the same one her father had purchased when he first opened and hadn't upgraded it since. With nothing but a small lobby area that held two chairs and an end table, her father's office, and a bathroom so small you had to sit on the toilet just to close the door, it was a strain for all of them to meet in the mornings.

Landon's '67 Chevy Nova sat in the lot along with Melody's Kia Forte, and her father's old beat-up Ford pickup.

"The whole gang's here." Hailey sighed.

The last thing she wanted to do was go inside and tell her family about her most recently failed relationship. Melody would look down on her and make comments that were seemingly harmless, yet would pack a powerful punch to Hailey's recently reduced level of self-esteem.

Landon, who wasn't part of the family at all, but a buff Navajo guy who wore his hair back in a ponytail and carried an axe on his belt, wouldn't even ask. He knew when to stay in his own lane.

The door to her father's office opened, catching Hailey's attention. An older man, wearing blue jeans and a western-style button-down shirt, stepped out. Slicking back his gray, thinning hair, he plopped a cowboy hat on top of it before it got away.

A client this early in the morning?

Her father rarely saw clients until after their morning meeting and everyone was out on assignment. The space was just not big enough for all of them and there was virtually no privacy. When all of them were there, one of them had to stand just to have a meeting. Landon usually gave up his seat no matter if he was there first or not. For all that he tried to play tough, he was a good guy.

The man tipped his hat and nodded as he passed by. Hailey nodded back and smiled. Watching him move through the small parking lot, she studied him, wondering if anything about him was familiar. Could this have something to do with her mother? And if it did, did Hailey really want to know?

A wave of nervousness washed over her as she continued to watch him in her side mirror, head to his truck, get in, and drive away.

Knock it off. You're just overreacting after seeing Rob — that was an image she refused to recreate in her head.

Now all she had to do was keep it from Melody. It wouldn't matter to her that Hailey hadn't known he was married. As soon as Melody heard about it, she would make Hailey feel like the screwup prodigal once again. It made no difference that Hailey had done the right thing about the situation as soon as she found out. Melody was constantly looking for a reason to criticize.

Melody poked her head out from inside the office and gave Hailey an impatient wave to come inside. Hailey sighed. It was too late to pull out of the parking lot, go home, cuddle up in her bed, and pretend the world was not cruel.

"Alright, alright, I'm coming." Hailey turned off her idling car and unbuckled her seatbelt. "Lord, keep me sane."

Now that Melody had seen her, there was no use trying to back out. Hailey sauntered up to the front door and pushed it open. The bell jingled as she went through, just like it had since she was a small child and she and her mother and sister would come up and bring their father dinner after a long night at work. Then after she disappeared, he'd become obsessed with finding her. So obsessed that he'd left his girls to play house while he searched high and low for a woman who did not want to be found.

Maybe she was being too hard on him. Noah Baker was a good man. He never deserved what their mother did to him, and neither did they. He'd done his best with what he had, and they had fared pretty well with little to no "mommy issues" to speak of.

The memory of those days was fading, though. Other than a few small reminders, like the bell around the door and a couple other known triggers, Hailey made a habit of not thinking about her mother at all. The woman had abandoned her family. Like it or not, in the dozen years since her departure, there was not one piece of evidence to prove an inkling of foul play. She was just… gone.

"Hurry up. Get in here. Dad has something important to talk to us about." Excitement lit Melody's face.

Landon stood. "Have a seat, Hails. I've been sitting all morning."

"What's going on?" Hailey took the offered seat, glanced at Landon, and gave him a smile of thanks before returning her attention to her sister.

"I don't know. That guy came in this morning to meet with Dad. I couldn't hear what they were saying but—"

"Translation—" Landon interrupted, standing against the wall next to Hailey. "She tried to hear what they were saying, but the walls in this hut are sounder than they look."

"Translation—" Melody countered, narrowing her eyes at Landon playfully. "I've never had to snoop on him before, so this must be important."

"What did Dad say?" Hailey folded her hands together, waiting.

"He said for everyone to stick around, is all," Melody answered.

"That's it?" Hailey asked.

"That's it," Landon grumbled, adjusting the ax on his hip. "I've got my assignment already. I'm tailing Carl Barnstreet today. His mother is just waiting to catch him cohabitating, so she can drop him like a hot potato."

"Carl Barnstreet?" Melody wrinkled her nose. "Cohabitating? Who would—"

"Oh, stop it." Hailey rolled her eyes. Melody was entirely too picky when it came to men. That was why she was twenty-seven and still single. Melody set high standards for herself and everyone else around her. If you didn't fit into her mold, you weren't doing things right. "Carl's an okay guy."

"He's a creep, and his mother should have stopped supporting him long ago."

Hailey was just about to dive in head-first with just how tired she was of her sister's arrogance when the door to the office opened, and their father peeked his head out.

"I'll need to see all three of you, please."

HAVE YOU READ THESE TITLES?

The Billionaire's London Bride

She's impulsive and outgoing. He's ... not.

Raven Hartly has been through a tremendous life-altering experience. When her best friend invites her on a week-long London vacation, she can't pack her bags fast enough. Set on getting away from reality, her only plan for the trip is to mindlessly enjoy herself.

Shy and reserved billionaire, Emmett Hunt is off to London to appease his older brother who is set on expanding the family business overseas. The idea is absurd, and Emmett would rather be doing anything else. His plan is to get in and get out, then go home and let his brother down easy.

When Raven and Emmett meet, their personalities couldn't be more different yet that only enhances their attraction to each other. But neither of them know how to get over the pain of their pasts.

Trigger Warning: Miscarriage

The Cowboy's Forbidden Bride

After the loss of her parents, Charlotte struggles to keep the family ranch going for her and her younger brother, Cole.

Ezra has a criminal past he'd like to escape, so when his boss pushes him too far, he runs despite the consequences.

When Cole rides up with a dying stranger strapped to the back of his horse, Charlotte recognizes the man she's met only once but never forgot. He doesn't want to put her life in danger, but he's too weak to leave.

She knows she needs to send him away to protect Cole and the ranch, but she'll do anything she can to keep him there...

The Act of Falling

Bekah, a singer at a local Long Beach night club, is a magnet for bad boys. When her boyfriend, Blade, gets arrested, she leaves everything behind, including her beloved guitar, to find something … else. Out of gas but with a plan, Bekah stops in the pristine little town of Sunshine, Arizona.

Ezekiel, the son of the town preacher, is also a teacher at the church's private school. He's quite content in his life and secure in his surroundings. Well, mostly … From the moment Bekah shows up in the church office, wearing a skirt shorter than a man's imagination, a hoop nose ring, and a tattoo of a spider on her back, Ezekiel's quiet little world shifts into territories unknown.

But no worries … she'll be gone by morning.

The Law of Falling

An officer of the law, a social worker, an ornery grandmother, and a flat tire.

When Samantha's grandmother takes a fall in her home, Samantha's parents worry she's not fit to live alone anymore. To her disdain, Samantha seems to have drawn the short straw and now must go out and evaluate her grandmother's situation.

It's only been a short time since Garrett has graduated from the police academy, and being a police officer is nothing like he'd thought. He is sorely missing the kids at the church where he used to teach. But when an attractive woman rolls into town with a flat tire, Garrett is intrigued with the newcomer.

Before they know it, Samantha and Garrett find themselves spending time together, and Gramma Matt may just be the cause of it...

The Billionaire's UnWelcome Home

A car crash reunited them, yet threatened to tear them apart.

After receiving word of his father's illness, Jesse James was hesitant to return home. He'd joined the military to get away from the billionaire and everything he stood for. But when his mother insisted he return, he conceded.

He was in no way prepared for what awaited him...

Monetarily, Maya's life couldn't be more perfect. Working for the James family, her son's every need was taken care of. That was, so long as she kept the family secret. But something was missing, and when Jesse showed up in town, Maya's life became much more complicated...

Love became a complication as Jesse and Maya fought for their right to become a family.

This is an interracial love story with racist themes.

Her Billionaire Dream

He's building an empire. She's cleaning it.

After years of reviving the family business from the ashes his father left, Chandler Jones has no time for a serious relationship. He has no need for companionship and only dates his high school sweetheart because she's equally rich, extremely independent, and looks good on his arm. But when she ducks out on him on the most important weekend of the year, Chandler is desperate.

Dena Gysler wants nothing to do with her rich, arrogant employer. She cleans his office, and he has no idea she exists which suits her just fine. When he offers her ten thousand dollars to accompany him to his weekend business conference, Dena is appalled. But ten thousand dollars is a lot of money for a cleaning lady to refuse.

Dena and Chandler agree to a strictly-business plan that will benefit them both. And falling in love is not a part of that plan.

But then again ... plans change.

To find out more about these characters and their lives check out the rest of the stories in this series.

Her Billionaire Jackpot — Max and Chloe — Mixed-up Marriage

Her Billionaire Wish — Zach and Chelsea — Cruise Ship Romance

Her Billionaire Chauffeur — Boss and Lara — Stranded Together

Her Billionaire Scoundrel — Jax and Jewel — Road Trip

Finding Alissa

When Alissa Martin finds out her fiancé is cheating on her, she's so distraught that she packs a suitcase and leaves. Too upset to think of anything but her fiancé's deception, she ends up in a car accident. Upon awakening in the hospital in the town of Trust, Arizona, she has lost her memory.

Already confused and frustrated, she is shocked when the stranger in her room tells her that she's a loving wife and mother of three.

Even after a year, Derek Andrews mourns the loss of his wife. But his wealthy father-in-law thinks it's time to move on. So much so, that he threatens to cut Derek off if he doesn't find a mother for the children. But could he ever love another woman?

When he comes upon the wreckage of a woman who looks identical to his Elle, he devises a scheme to make her a part of their family...

To find out more about these characters and their lives check out the rest of the stories in this series.

Loving Josie — A Rags to Riches Story

Reclaiming Bailey — A Second Chances Story

Chasing Kennedy — An Online Love Story

To read these and more click on Tayla Alexandra's Author Page to see her full list of books.

GET FREE BOOKS AND EXCLUSIVE TAYLA ALEXANDRA MATERIAL

Connecting with readers is one of the greatest things about writing. I send a weekly newsletter with details on new releases, special offers, and other news tidbits related to my writing.

By signing up for my mailing list, not only will you get exclusive insider news, I'll send you the following titles for free in your choice of Kindle, ePub, or pdf versions

To Trust Again, A Novella

Brother of the Bride, A novelette

Wrapped in Love, A Christmas short

Sign up here[1] for exclusive member access and your free ebooks.

---

1. https://dl.bookfunnel.com/ptrgwt4xc4

ABOUT THE AUTHOR

Tayla Alexandra is the author of Her Sweet Billionaire Romance Series, Finding Trust Romance Series among several others. She makes her online home at Tayla Alexandra Books. You can connect with Tayla on Twitter, on Facebook , and you can send an email at TAlexandraAuthor@gmail.com

facebook.com/talexandraromance
twitter.com/AlexandraTayla
amazon.com/author/taylaalexandra
bookbub.com/profile/tayla-alexandra